Praise for Scottie Barrett's *Carnal Deceptions*

5 Stars! Sensuality Rating: Sizzling *"Carnal Deceptions* is a compelling ugly duckling story of revenge, jealousy, danger, and deceit. Tess is a heroine that many readers will applaud, while Tallon is an incomparable hero many women would love to call their own....if you like lush, red hot love scenes, be sure to pick this one up."

~ *Lettetia, Ecataromance Sensual*

Look for these titles by
Scottie Barrett

Now Available:

The Viscount's Addiction

Coming Soon:

The Moss Rose

Carnal Deceptions

Scottie Barrett

A SAMHAIN PUBLISHING, LTD. publication.

Samhain Publishing, Ltd.
577 Mulberry Street, Suite 1520
Macon, GA 31201
www.samhainpublishing.com

Carnal Deceptions
Copyright © 2008 by Scottie Barrett
Print ISBN: 978-1-59998-815-3
Digital ISBN: 1-59998-601-9

Editing by Linda Ingmanson
Cover by Scott Carpenter

First Samhain Publishing, Ltd. electronic publication: September 2007
First Samhain Publishing, Ltd. print publication: July 2008

Prologue

Tess's foot caught in the hem of her dress. Wet from the cemetery lawn, her skirt now dragged the ground. She imagined tendrils of fog wrapping around her ankles, pulling her back toward her father's grave. Beadle's hand at her elbow steadied her before she could fall headlong into the carriage.

The horses set a somber pace as they traveled down the road. The weeping willows that narrowed the path to Tess's home scraped against the sides of the carriage. With his cane, Beadle lifted a corner of the curtain. "The vultures have gathered again. They'll pick it clean before the day is out. Shame on Sloan and his shady ventures."

The debt collectors were clustered like undertakers around a dead house. She clutched her trembling hands together. How would she work up the courage to walk past them? For comfort, she slipped her hand into her reticule and rubbed the stone once. It always felt as though it had just been plucked from the river, as cool as when she'd first removed it from her father's pocket.

Beadle rapped the roof of the carriage hard with his cane. She jolted back against the seat as the horses lurched forward. Unthinkingly, she grabbed at Beadle's arm. He gave her a cunning, sidelong glance, and she quickly released it.

"I doubted you had any great wish to pay a visit to Fleet Prison. I do not think those collectors will find enough in that empty farmhouse to satisfy your father's debts. And they'll come looking for more." Beadle settled back into the corner of the carriage and stared at her, his lips quirked in an odd, condescending smile. "The one piece of property not entailed was your father's house in town. Naturally, he bequeathed it to you. Selling it may help remedy the situation. But it will take some time to dispose of, located as it is in such an unfashionable part of London. In the meantime, I've found a situation for you that will keep you from their clutches." As he said the last, his tone took on a melodramatic timbre.

Before she could reply, he tossed something into the lap of her borrowed mourning gown. She swallowed a scream. Mice! She quickly pulled her hands away to avoid touching them.

Her startled movement didn't send them scurrying as it should have. She took a closer look. Not mice, just fur. Actually, commas of fur.

"Your coloring, my dear, is so loud it announces you from across the street." From below the seat he pulled out a hatbox and removed a drab, brown wig. "You'll wear this, and these—" with his long, delicate fingers he lifted one of the fur commas "—are for your brows."

What on earth was the man suggesting? Could she truly be in danger of landing in debtor's prison? Though she hadn't felt the need to wear stays beneath the vast dress she wore, she felt as though she couldn't take a deep breath. The moldy odor of the rented cab and the damp wool smell of Beadle's coat made the air thick and suffocating.

He tugged on a coil of her hair and released it. The curl sprung back. When her father was alive, the man would never have dared lay a finger on her. She pressed herself against the wall.

"Copper hair, pale green eyes—can't disappear into the wallpaper with those attributes." Beadle said it as if she'd painted herself purposefully in garish shades as a prostitute might. "And whatever you do, do not smile."

Her face felt stiff from tears, the instinct to smile a memory. She put her fingers to her lips, wondering what he found so offensive about her smile.

He seemed to read her thoughts. "It gives a man ideas whether he wants them or not," he said resentfully.

What ideas? She did not want to pursue the question.

"Lady Stadwell has promised to take you on. I haven't told her everything, of course. She's suffered, too. Sloan swindled her husband, as well. When Lord Stadwell died, she was forced to move from Crossfield Hall to the dowager house. The poor dear is living in very reduced circumstances."

Tess wished she had the courage to ask if Lady Stadwell had also been fooled into taking Beadle's advice.

"If your father hadn't been so damned greedy for your future, you'd be safely married by now. The viscount turned down every suitable offer."

Tess had a deep suspicion he had been one of those asking for her hand. Her cheeks felt on fire. She rubbed the odd, furry eyebrows between her fingers. Her throat tightened, but she refused to cry.

"Coupling with a man of business wasn't bloody good enough for his daughter." He'd turned his face and muttered this, but she'd heard every revolting word. He placed his hand on her thigh. She stiffened. "Facing ruination, I suppose you would be happy for any man to make an offer now."

She peeled his hand off her leg. "I'll be happiest if I'm left alone." How dare the man take such liberties? Her father had left him in charge of the estate, not her future. Tess shrank into the corner. Brave thoughts indeed, but she had no one but Beadle to depend on.

He bared his teeth in a not so pleasant smile. "My dear, the decision may not be yours to make."

Chapter One

"'Tis the devil's own."

Startled, Tess stopped digging in the soil and sat back on her heels. She glanced over to see if Lady Stadwell had been muttering in her sleep. But she was very much awake. Her pale blue eyes squinted into the distance. The sunlight streaming through the latticed gazebo cast a diamond pattern across her cheeks.

Tess, hearing the clatter of hooves, turned her attention to the drive. She assumed Lady Stadwell was talking about the horse. The huge, black brute snorted and rolled its eyes as if possessed. It took her only a moment to notice the rider. His unfashionably long hair was the same glossy, midnight black as the horse's coat. His greatcoat flapped threateningly with each muscled stride of the animal.

Tess found herself holding her breath, until she remembered she was invisible.

The man reined in the horse and shouted at the groom, "Stand clear, man. The beast is liable to leave his hoof print on your forehead." Dismounting, he snatched the bridle and delivered the horse to the stables on his own.

Lady Stadwell re-draped her shawl, tweaked the curls at her temples and pinched her cheeks for color just as if she were expecting a beau. Her eyes flitted anxiously in the direction of the stables, and Tess, finding herself curious, watched as the man vaulted the garden fence. He landed with a soft thud beside the blue hydrangea bushes.

He strode past her, his coat brushing her arm. There was the slightest hitch in his gait as though one leg troubled him.

The instant he greeted Lady Stadwell, Tess knew with certainty he was the devil she spoke of. He looked quite apart from Lady Stadwell's usual visitors. His hair was somewhat ragged on the ends. A thin white scar bisected one of his black brows. There were no jewels on his fingers or foppish ruffles at his wrist or neck. His heavy black boots were scuffed and dust covered, like a workingman's. It brought to mind her father's boots caked with mud and left on the porch step after a day in the fields. Her father, who had been heir to a noble title, a rundown estate and little else, had turned to farming for a living.

"So you've ascended, Nephew."

"I have," he said, and bestowed a kiss on one of her gloved hands.

"And where are your minions?"

"They've grown wearisome. I suggested they remain behind."

So this was the infamous Earl of Marcliffe. Tess had heard much about Lady Stadwell's notorious nephew. Servant and *ton* alike discussed his exploits. Always out of earshot of Lady Stadwell, of course. But Tess, being invisible, had overheard all. Women were said to make fools of themselves for a chance in his bed. It was rumored that a duel initiated by a cuckolded husband had ended in death. Tess surmised that he'd joined the army to get away from his black reputation.

Lord Marcliffe did not look anything like the man Tess had imagined, a man who'd wear his decadence proudly. And, with surprise, she noted that his aunt had a great affection for him. Lady Stadwell's acerbic wit rarely surfaced; she saved it for the select few she was genuinely fond of.

He sprawled onto the seat opposite his aunt. Tall, with impossibly broad shoulders, he looked ridiculous on the dainty wrought iron bench. He stretched his long legs in front of him, crossing them at the ankle. His booted feet came to rest beside his aunt's pink kidskin slippers. Lady Stadwell's feet, which Tess had never remarked as being overly small, looked like they belonged to a child next to his.

Tess fingered the residue of the daffodil bulbs he'd crushed underfoot as he'd strode past her crouched figure. Like most of Lady Stadwell's guests, he hadn't noticed her, so Tess felt free to take his measure. She'd become quite accustomed to being overlooked. In truth, she preferred to be ignored than to hear the cruel comments of Lady Stadwell's friends. Only yesterday, Lady Trenton, waiting until Lady Stadwell bustled out of the room to fetch her snuffbox, wondered aloud how her friend didn't fall into a state of gloom having to look at "that mourning-garbed crow" every day. Not to be outdone, Mrs. Barton had said, with a sly cat-eyed glance in Tess's direction and a badly muffled yawn, "I think she's become part of the furnishings." And the men, they simply avoided looking at her, maneuvering around her like a yellowing, water-stained statue.

In this instance, for reasons she could not name, Tess found she did not want to be taken for granted. "I'm afraid, Lady Stadwell, we will have a poor showing of blooms," she blurted.

He turned to look at her for the first time, rubbing his shadowed jaw with his forefinger and thumb. The gesture was simple enough, but Tess found it strangely appealing.

Pinching the fragments of broken bulbs, she sprinkled the

13

ground with them. "Clod," she muttered under her breath.

"What's that you say?" He sat forward, his hands clasped, his arms resting on his spread thighs. Tess couldn't help noticing that he even sat like a man, not a dandified aristocrat.

"You, my lord, are careless. Do you have any idea what trouble it was to get these bulbs?" Even as the words left her mouth, she wondered where on earth she would get another position.

She took some comfort in Lady Stadwell's tittering laugh and yet she continued watching his dark blue eyes for reaction. Surprisingly, rather than dismissing her on the spot, he smiled. But she did not feel relieved. Rather she was left with the odd sensation of having lost something...or of having had it stolen. Amazing, all this time she'd thought her heart impervious.

"I do hope I didn't step on your fingers," he said with a gentleness Tess found hard to reconcile with his rough appearance.

"No, you managed to miss them," she said.

His brows lifted at her sarcasm. He turned back to his aunt. "Who's the girl?"

"Hortensia Calloway. Your uncle's man of business suggested she would suit me as a companion. I must say she is very good at keeping me out of trouble." Lady Stadwell chuckled. "Hiring her was the excuse I needed to send my sister on her way. You would not believe the dusty tomes she'd force me to listen to, and she would never allow me fresh air unless I was swaddled like an infant." For emphasis, she plucked at the tassels of the thin, impractical shawl she now wore.

"So, you still have dealings with Beadle?"

"As you well know, I haven't any wealth left to require his advice. But he did help to straighten out my affairs after Alfred's death. I believe he was quite blameless in that dreadful matter."
14

"Of that I have never been convinced."

"But then, Nephew, you do have a mistrustful nature."

Tess braced herself on one hand and stabbed the ground with her trowel. She was not convinced of Beadle's innocence either. Doubts about him had plagued her since her father's fall from grace. With frustration, she blew at the copper-colored strands of hair that had worked their way from beneath her wig then realized with a start that her disguise might be compromised. Granted, Lady Stadwell's eyesight was poor. She hadn't even noticed the other morning when Tess had left off wearing the powder that paled her lashes into nonexistence. But somehow Tess was certain that Lord Marcliffe's eyes were not only beautiful but keen. And she knew exactly how he saw her. As drab Hortensia. She winced as she yanked out the stray red-gold hairs.

How she hated the disguise. The wig itched unbearably. The clothing was bulky and of such a depressingly faded color that it brought her to tears to see herself in the mirror. Once again, she cursed Rowland Beadle for insisting on this ridiculous costume. Yet she couldn't completely hate the man. He had made certain her father had been buried in hallowed ground, squelching rumors of suicide. And he'd saved her from the hell of debtor's prison.

Lady Stadwell made a clicking sound with her tongue. "No one would ever gather from your appearance, Marcliffe, that you are an earl. You look worse than a farmer."

Deeply offended, Tess felt the need to interject, "My father was a farmer."

His eyes seemed to assess her again.

"I am forever telling the girl that she will never interest any man with that blunt tongue," Lady Stadwell told her nephew.

Tess smiled to herself. Lady Stadwell was eternally

15

optimistic about her chances of finding a mate, not seeming to realize that it would take a rare man, indeed, to be interested. A man who held no stock in pleasing physical attributes or wealth. Though, judging by Lady Stadwell's youthful portraits, she had definitely not been a beauty, and she'd managed to marry. Of course, she'd had a hefty dowry to recommend her.

Lady Stadwell tilted her head and narrowed her eyes as she scrutinized her nephew. "My dear boy, why don't you trim your hair? You'd be far more handsome."

He simply smiled and shrugged. For the first time Tess noticed the dimple. A far too charming indentation in his left cheek. Any more handsome, she thought wryly, and the man would melt stone.

"And to what do I owe this privileged visit?" Lady Stadwell asked with a coy bat of her lashes.

With a crooked grin, he tugged a piece of paper from the pocket of his waistcoat. "'Marcliffe, my dear boy, it is urgent that you come. No less than life or death'," he read, laughter underlying his tone.

"I'd forgotten I'd written that little missive." Abruptly, Lady Stadwell's voice turned serious. "The blackguard's back in town. Throwing banknotes around quite liberally. And despite that vulgar display, he is all the rage. Beatrice encountered him at Lady Trenton's party."

"I was aware the damn fool had returned. Amazing that he is spending some of his own blunt. He usually depends on his friends to carry him." Lord Marcliffe rubbed his thigh.

"He's a fool all right. But at least he was smart enough not to get himself skewered by a Frenchman." Lady Stadwell glanced pointedly at his leg.

"The only injury that bastard faced was a sore wrist from holding up cards. He spent the whole of the war in the gambling hells." He tapped his thigh a moment, his brow furrowing the tiniest bit. "Besides, nothing missing here. The limb's just a little stubborn. And it wasn't a skewer, more like a slice."

Lady Stadwell grimaced. "Please, Nephew, spare us the details."

What a cryptic conversation, Tess thought. Who was this blackguard? Tess stood and brushed off her hands. "It's time for your tea, my lady." Far better to be doing something useful than to be lurking here, mesmerized by a midnight blue gaze. Her eyes skated over to him again. She pinched the inside of her wrist to bring herself back to reality. She was acting a complete idiot.

She refused to walk in front of him to give him an eyeful of her shapeless form. Instead, she circled wide around the gazebo. Grabbing up her skirts with her filthy hands, she lifted her chin in a ridiculously haughty manner and marched out of the garden. She winced, knowing that she was trampling the seedlings she'd painstakingly planted only a week before. *Please don't let him stay long,* she implored, to what entity she did not know.

The front door was constructed of thick, blackened oak. Tess needed both hands and all her strength to open it. As it creaked open, Lady Stadwell's two massive hounds slammed into her, rocking her backward. Losing her balance, she fell on her bottom.

The mastiffs looked as formidable as lions as they bounded across the courtyard and over the lawn. She'd never seen the dogs move with such alacrity. On chilly days, they might move from the base of the divan by their mistress's skirts to the great, stone fireplace. When they'd absorbed enough of the heat, they would lumber back to their mistress. And on unseasonably warm days, they would lie on the cool marble of the front hall, quite effectively obstructing the entryway.

Tess scrambled to her feet, watching with awe, as the huge dogs pushed through the narrow garden opening, barking with excitement. At full gallop, they raced at Lord Marcliffe. It was a wonder they didn't knock him flat. He gave them affectionate rubs. The silly creatures, looking like overgrown pups, tried to nudge each other out of the way to get the earl's attention. Apparently, even animals found the man fascinating.

Once inside, Tess strolled down the long corridor, taking time to admire all the paintings lining the walls. She stopped and fiddled with the flowers she'd arranged that very morning. She plucked a few petals from the yellow roses that looked a bit on the tired side. With the sleeve of her sweater, she polished a tiny blemish on the wood table. She could have crawled and gotten there sooner, she thought, as she finally entered the kitchen. Perhaps if she dawdled long enough the man would be gone before the tea was even poured.

The kitchen was empty. Tess surmised that Mrs. Smith, the cook, was ailing from rheumatism again. Only a few devoted servants, most of them elderly, had chosen to stay with Lady Stadwell when her fortunes plummeted. Having indulged in too much sherry one evening, Lady Stadwell had confided in Tess about her husband's financial mishaps and the vile man who had absconded with well-nigh half their wealth.

That night Tess found a kindred spirit, someone who lived for the same thing: *revenge.* Was it possible Sloan was the man Lady Stadwell and her nephew spoke of just now? Hatred pulsed through Tess as she thought of the man who had ruined her father, the man who had obliterated her chance for happiness.

Tess poured water into the basin and scoured her hands with the rough soap. After fetching a kettle from the stove, she went out the kitchen door to the pump. She applied delicate pressure and a piddling amount of water plinked into the kettle.

She concentrated again on wishing Lord Marcliffe away. The man disturbed her immensely. Thankfully, he did not strike her as the kind of man who would stay overlong in one place. A quick visit with his aunt, and then he'd be back on that monstrous beast of his, thundering down the drive.

"I think I could have grown the tea in the time it has taken you to set the water to boil."

The deep voice unsettled her completely and she dropped the kettle. She bent over the barrel to retrieve it, her face flushing hot. "Blasted," she cursed under her breath.

He leaned negligently against the doorframe. "Can I help?"

Yes, by leaving, she wanted to say. She peered up at him shyly from beneath her pale, powdered lashes and shook her head. He loomed in the doorway. His shoulders nearly spanned the opening. She took a steadying breath. She'd never met a man so intensely masculine and so completely at ease in his own skin.

He stepped outside. "She is fiddling with her rings. I was afraid she might twist a finger off."

Tess smiled, amazed that he'd actually noticed his aunt's little quirk. Patience was not one of Lady Stadwell's virtues. Tess worked the pump more vigorously now, but obviously not fast enough as far as he was concerned. He put his big hand atop hers and pushed down. With a gasp she yanked her hand away. Water from the kettle sloshed onto her apron.

"Scared little rabbit, aren't you?" He took the kettle from her.

She cradled the hand he'd touched. The odd, shivering sensation she'd felt the instant he'd placed his hand on hers was just beginning to fade.

Scottie Barrett

"I don't bite, really." His rather dangerous smile said otherwise.

Her eyes narrowed as she scrutinized him. "I think perhaps you do."

Surprisingly, her barb amused him. His laugh had a hoarse catch to it. To her dismay, Tess found it an altogether pleasing sound.

"Well, at least, not on first acquaintance."

At the thought of his teeth scraping gently over her skin, a scintillating tingle ran up her spine.

He finished filling the kettle. Tess followed him inside. His boots sounded heavy on the tile flooring as he walked to the stove. There was the slightest shuffling sound accompanying each successive step.

After setting the kettle on the flame he turned to her. "Your eyes are an uncommon green. I don't think I've ever seen their like."

"Rather like gooseberries, I imagine." With trembling hands, she took the tin of biscuits from the cupboard. Quite extraordinary that he noticed her eyes. Certainly he was merely taking pity on a poor, homely creature. She plucked two cups from the cupboard and set them with a rattle atop their matching saucers.

"I'm amazed my aunt has any china left at all."

Tess frowned at her awkwardness. She prided herself on her culinary skills. She could fashion elaborate tarts and cakes, handle tiny candied violets, draw fanciful designs with icing, but this morning her hands were like claws. *'Tis naught but a simple cup of tea,* she chided herself.

She skirted around him, accidentally brushing his wool coat with the back of her hand. Her hands were visibly shaking

20

now, and she yanked the drawer of the tea caddy too hard. The tea flew out, scenting the air with jasmine and powdering her apron with tealeaves. She sneezed.

"You are truly the clumsiest chit I've ever met," he said with a chuckle.

She lowered her lashes in a most obsequious manner. "Sorry to be keeping you. I'm sure a man of your stature has many urgent matters to attend to." In her mind, she ticked off all the things he could occupy himself with: seducing women, cutting a debauched swathe through London, managing his huge estate, counting his fortune and of course actually bedding those many women he seduced. Why, she fretted, did the idea of him finding pleasure in bed seem to be uppermost on her mind?

He stood close enough to her that their images were cast in the kettle. Granted, the kettle had a deforming effect on both their features. But her haggish reflection gave her the shudders. Why had she stopped at this point in her disguise? Wouldn't a wart have been just the touch she needed? It was a little like the beauty and the beast. No she wasn't being realistic. It was exactly like it.

"If I didn't know any better, I would say you are hoping to be rid of me soon." He dusted the tea flakes from his lapels. His dark blue eyes considered her for a long, uncomfortable moment. "How long have you been acquainted with Beadle?" The question pretended to be one of polite interest. He even lifted the corners of his lips, but he wasn't really smiling.

Stupidly, she hadn't even questioned why he'd deigned to speak to her. Now it was perfectly clear. The man was suspicious of her.

"My father had business dealings with him."

"Curious. A farmer in need of a man of business."

"Yes, even we dirt poor peasants require help investing our farthings."

He acknowledged her sarcasm with a half smile. "Perhaps if you know Beadle then you are also acquainted with Sloan, his oft times associate."

At the mention of the hated name, her hands curled into fists, fingernails digging into her palms. "I did not make it a habit of mingling with my father's business associates," she said in a constricted tone.

One of his well-shaped black brows quirked skeptically. "With the exception of Beadle, that is. Rather uncommon for an advisor to take such an interest in a client's daughter."

"What exactly are you implying, Lord Marcliffe?" She swallowed, determined not to cry in front of him or give him a clue as to her true identity, as Beadle had advised. She had suffered too long in this humiliating disguise to give it all away with a few ridiculous tears.

He shrugged his broad shoulders. "Merely an observation."

Lady Stadwell had the right of it. He was as seductive as the devil—as clever, too, it seemed. If she wasn't careful, she would find herself confessing all of her deepest secrets. Though it occurred to Tess that serving a debtor's sentence might be less painful than living this lie.

"Now, if you will excuse me, I will see to Lady Stadwell." She picked up the tray and hurried off like the scared rabbit he thought her.

Chapter Two

Bloody grand. The man was staying for dinner. She comforted herself with the notion that Lady Stadwell would certainly not invite her to dine on such a special occasion. Tess was determined to stay well clear of the dining hall. But, to her dismay, Lady Stadwell rang her imperious bell, and she found herself summoned to a place at the table.

"He's gone to check that great beast of his," Lady Stadwell said. She'd been waiting mere moments, but she was already restive, fidgeting with the rings on her fingers.

Tess's trembling hands were equally occupied. She'd been folding and refolding her napkin from the moment she'd sat down. Lady Stadwell shifted in her seat and heaved dramatic sighs as time drew on.

"He is quite handsome, is he not?" Lady Stadwell asked suddenly, piercing the silence.

Struck dumb by the question, Tess concentrated on reshaping her napkin yet again.

"Hortensia, did you not hear me? For goodness sakes, stop torturing that piece of linen."

Tess dropped the napkin and stared down at her place setting. "Yes, yes indeed he is handsome—in that muscular, rugged, godlike sort of way." It was then she wished she'd made better use of her napkin by shoving it into her overlarge mouth.

Lady Stadwell said nothing at first. Then she picked up her own napkin and pressed it to her lips. The cloth did little to muffle her amusement. Tess could do nothing but laugh along with her.

When the door opened, Lord Marcliffe entered, the fresh, cold scent of the outdoors lingering on him. "Sorry to have kept you waiting."

What had they been laughing at, *really*? Her description of the man could not have been more accurate.

Lord Marcliffe did not seem surprised to see a hired companion dining with his aunt, which helped to relieve some of Tess's nervousness. He settled his big frame onto the chair across from her. It was impossible not to notice that his hair and clothes were a bit disheveled.

"Tallon, is everything all right?" Lady Stadwell asked.

"Everything is fine, Aunt." He made a casual attempt at combing his hair back with his fingers. "That wood out by the stables, is that being used for anything?" he asked nonchalantly.

"Not that I know of. What would you need it for?"

"Oh, nothing really." He picked up his wine goblet and took a few hearty swigs. "A little hole is all. Just needs a little reinforcement."

"Heavens, Tallon, did that monster do something to my stables?"

"Nothing that can't be remedied with a little wood and nails." He finished off the wine in his glass. There was a hint of amusement in his eyes. "Oh, and your driving mare may be expecting a foal next spring."

"Do you mean to tell me that beast got ahold of old Matty? My heavens, she must have been so traumatized."

Tess blushed at the turn the conversation had taken.

"No." His sly smile evolved into a devastating grin. "I don't think *traumatized* would be the word."

Tess giggled behind her hand, and he threw a conspiratorial wink her way.

Lady Stadwell emitted a snort of disgust. "All males, no matter the species, are darned predictable."

"Do you think the same, Miss Calloway?" he asked.

Tess stopped and stared at him, her fork halfway to her mouth. "Y-Yes," she answered truthfully. Though her experience with men was completely tame, her short London season had exposed her to some tiresome courting rituals. Boasting was a particularly annoying habit of her suitors. Lord Kempstone, her most ardent pursuer, had managed to steer every conversation to his hunting conquests.

She recalled with humor Kempstone proudly presenting her with a sack full of grouse in the middle of an elegant soiree. Her lips curled up in the full-on teeth-revealing smile that her father had found enchanting and likened to the impact of a room lit with a thousand candles. "Tone everything down," Beadle had warned her. "Think of yourself as wallpaper."

Her fingers flew to cover her mouth. It was a ridiculous gesture she knew. This man wouldn't show an interest in her even if she climbed atop the table and danced. She chanced a look at his eyes to test her theory and found his gaze riveted on her. She was inventing things. He only stared at her like that because she'd just pronounced men predictable animals.

He looked at her quizzically for a moment more, and then his attention drifted back to his meal. He sawed at his slice of beef. Tess was certain he was used to food that melted in his mouth. Mrs. Smith had taken to soaking cuts of meat in a wine concoction. But not even alcohol could help to tenderize this gristly meal.

He chewed it with consternation, furrowing his brow, the strong muscles in his jaw working hard. He was giving it a valiant try. "Hell's fire, what sort of animal was this? Or is it tree bark? I ought to send you my cook."

With difficulty, Tess swallowed back her laughter.

Lady Stadwell shooed away his offer with a flick of her hand. "Predictable as well, Nephew. How often have you suggested that? Five times, at least. And it's that predictability that has given me an ingenious notion."

Lord Marcliffe set down his knife and fork, sat back in his chair and folded his arms across his chest. "What notion?" he asked, skepticism in every syllable.

Lady Stadwell took a slow sip of her wine, obviously enjoying her nephew's full attention. She set the glass down with a peculiar smile. "When you and Captain Gibbs went off to battle, where do you think your Cambridge classmate, Sloan, was? Safely ensconced in White's placing bets on the war's outcome, that's where. He must have felt a true coward when you two returned as heroes. I'm convinced he wanted to injure your pride when he tried to woo that little bedmate of yours. Too bad for him that she is so devoted to you."

Tess blushed at the reference to his mistress and averted her eyes, trying to focus on something else in the room. It suddenly did not feel the least bit appropriate that she be there.

"Who the devil told you all that?" Lord Marcliffe asked.

"I am not at liberty to say."

"Gibbs. What a bloody big mouth." He held up his hand. "Pray, do not list anymore details of my life. Tell me, instead, what you are contemplating in that devious mind of yours."

She responded to her nephew's irritation with an innocent

blink of her eyes. "Fine. I will discuss what I've gleaned about Sloan instead. Did you know his last mistress was privy to his schemes? And that she imparted the information to another man—a lover Sloan was apparently unaware of. Her disloyalty saved that lover his fortune. He was probably the only investor lucky enough to come out of that scheme with his hide intact. I suggest we let Sloan lure Miss Sparkes from you this time. And, because *he is a man,* he will predictably share confidences across the pillow. Then we can catch him before he strikes again."

He gave a hoarse, sarcastic bark of a laugh. "You cannot be serious."

"Perfectly serious. I will see him in prison before I die. Tallon, I do believe you are being terribly selfish. You should gladly share that girl of yours for this noble purpose."

Tess busied herself with the jerky-like meat on her plate and pretended not to be listening, but she was absorbing every word about Sloan. When the room went suddenly quiet, she glanced up to find Lord Marcliffe watching her.

"I wonder, Aunt, if we should continue this discussion after we eat."

"I am perfectly comfortable letting Hortensia hear about my plans. Now what of it? Will you help snare Sloan?"

He gave Tess another assessing look before responding to his aunt. "Did you think I'd intended to let this slide? I've had men tracking Sloan for months now. So far he has been the perfect citizen, but that won't last. A man who traffics in lies and bribes will not lay low for long. And when he shows his hand, I will be there."

"All well and good, but we will apply both measures to destroying him. If you don't feel like sharing your mistress, we will go about hiring one of her sort."

"I wonder that those he has swindled have not exposed him," Tess interjected.

There was a glimmer of suspicion in his eyes again. Clearly, her connection to Beadle made him mistrustful. He hesitated a moment before replying. "He wisely swindles those worried enough about social position, those who would never admit to touching anything smacking of trade or profit. It ensures their silence. I've heard that a couple of the men he'd duped resorted to taking their own lives rather than face the humiliation of it all."

His last sentence caused her to nearly choke on her food. The need for revenge flowed fresh and hot, flooding Tess's heart, making it burst with hatred. If only she could be the woman who would bring Sloan to his knees.

"Are you not well, Miss Calloway? You look a bit shaken."

The man was positively hawk-eyed. "I'm fine," she said.

"It will work," Lady Stadwell said, picking up on the unfinished argument. "You are just too stubborn to credit me with a workable plan."

"And what am I to do? Haunt the local brothels until I find the perfect woman? Actually that is not an unappealing idea."

"Don't be coarse, Nephew. I am serious." She made a sweet attempt at being forceful by hitting her frail fist on the table. "We can advertise. Discreetly, of course."

"And what should the advertisement read? Needing to hire a beautiful, duplicitous woman to spy?"

"Subtlety was never your strongest attribute. Do not be so narrow in your thinking, Tallon. Sometimes unconventional means have more success."

ℂ

When Mrs. Smith suggested that Tess take the breakfast tray to Lord Marcliffe, she was only too willing to comply.

Tess wanted to know whether the earl was actually considering his aunt's plan of revenge. But, in truth, that motive did not come close to explaining her eagerness to see the man, especially since she'd resolved to avoid him. Nor did it explain why she had lain awake until the early morning listening for his distinctive step. The one heavy footfall followed soon after by a more lingering chafing sound.

All night, she'd tortured herself with questions of his whereabouts. Was he exploring the brothels of London? Or had he bedded his mistress, the one his aunt so callously suggested he share with Sloan? At one point, she tried to imagine what it would be like to be his lover. Lying stark naked on a bed of satin, submitting to all of his erotic demands. She had found herself so dizzy from the mere thought of having him touch her bare skin, she'd had to splash her face with cold water. Even now, as she opened his door, she had to slow her erratic breathing.

Tess should have feared entering his lair. Instead, she relished the notion of waking him. She shut the door with a bang.

The room was heavy with darkness and the thick scent of liquor. Flinging back the drapes, she was disappointed by the thin light the gray day let in. She set the tray by his bed with a clatter. She clinked the spoon against the empty china cup. With satisfaction, she saw his dark eyelashes flutter, and then with a grunt, he opened one lazy lid and squinted at her. He raised himself onto his elbows and with some considerable effort, he managed a seated position. He shoved a tangle of black hair out of his face and scowled at her.

29

"I was sleeping," he said, his voice a scratchy remnant of its usual deep timbre.

"Your aunt requested that I bring you your breakfast. It is, after all, past noon."

He swung his legs over the edge of the bed and scrubbed his face with his hands. "Christ," he grumbled and threw off the sheets. He walked fully naked across the room. Tess stepped backward, caught her foot on the carpet and tottered for a moment before steadying herself on the bedpost.

She stared at the Persian rug, too embarrassed to look at him.

"Sweeting, when a woman enters a man's bedroom uninvited, he can only assume she's quite comfortable with what she might find behind a closed door."

The man obviously had no scruples when it came to women. "L-Lord Marcliffe, I believe you take pleasure in shocking. Do you do this to every unsuspecting maid fool enough to enter your room?"

"Actually, you seem to be the *only* female fool enough to enter when I am clearly asleep. I've had a long night."

"Yes, you have," she muttered under her breath.

"What's that you say?" He could not possibly have heard her, yet he now walked decidedly toward her. Tess was too petrified to move. He stopped directly in front of her. Heat radiated from his skin.

"Would you like to know what I was doing all night, Miss Calloway?" His voice was rough and suggestive. He was a cold-hearted devil who obviously gave no thought to a woman's feelings.

Emboldened by his rudeness, she lifted her gaze. Amazingly, he looked even bigger unclothed. He seemed to fill the enormous room, to take up all its air. Tess felt as though she were suffocating. She wondered if the women he bedded found him as formidable a figure as she did. "I have about as much interest in your nightly exploits as I have in a tomcat's. I am sorry that I woke you, but I was doing your aunt's bidding."

"From now on, it would behoove you to do mine. I take my coffee black."

Pretending to be the obedient servant, Tess returned to the tray and discreetly dropped a couple of lumps of sugar in his coffee. From behind her, she heard the lid of his cheroot box being lifted. In moments, the rich scent of tobacco competed with the pervasive odor of alcohol. She swiveled on her heels hoping to make a quick exit before he had the chance to humiliate her again.

Her eyes betrayed her, straying to his naked form. He was staring at her, the cheroot clamped between his smirking lips. Her hand flew to her mouth, but not before the gasp had escaped it. She quickly averted her eyes.

"You could give a man doubts." He'd seen where she'd been looking or at least the direction her gaze had wandered.

Her reaction had not been an assessment of his manhood...or to be precise not only of his manhood. The man was powerfully proportioned everywhere, it seemed. However, it was the ugly arcing scar that seamed his thigh that truly shocked her.

"That was from a saber?" she asked. It looked more to her like the work of a vicious shark. It was jagged and puckered. She wondered if the war had damaged him on the inside as well as the outside. Perhaps that was why he lived outside the moral boundaries of society. Of course, there was always the chance he'd been born defiant. There were always individuals who felt rules did not apply to them.

"Not a saber." He crossed the room toward her, and she stared down at the rug. She heard the bed creak. "You needn't hide your eyes any longer, Miss Calloway. I'm covered."

She risked a glance. The bedclothes were draped haphazardly over his lap, his eyes were narrowed against the spiral of smoke wending toward the plaster cherubs gracing the ceiling. She noticed that his shoulder had been similarly scored with a blade.

"The Frenchman I was lucky enough to meet had no use for such sophisticated weaponry. He carried an implement more suited to butchery."

"Lady Stadwell was right. Mr. Sloan was clever to have stayed away from the war."

"Curious that you mention him. You find criminals interesting, do you?" The sneer that slanted his lips unnerved her.

"How could I not be curious? There are days Lady Stadwell speaks of little else," she answered as she hurried to escape.

"And was it curiosity that brought you into my bedroom uninvited?"

His laughter chased her down the hall.

Chapter Three

Lady Stadwell stopped at the large window and stared out at the drive before sitting for breakfast. Flanked on each side by a big dog, she appeared to suppress a smile as she lowered herself onto the chair.

The flattened nap of the rug showed Lady Stadwell's well-trodden path to the window. A week had passed since the earl's departure, and every day Tess prayed he wouldn't return, and every night alone in bed she chided herself for a liar. One thing to be grateful for, she found that her sudden clumsiness had faded with his absence. For the time being, Lady Stadwell's porcelain was safe.

"You look to be in good spirits this morning, my lady." Tess immediately began preparing a plate for her.

"That I am. 'Tis a lovely day."

Tess glanced out at the cheerless weather.

"I have reason to believe my nephew will return today. It should take no more than two days to secure his house and take care of unfinished business. Reckoning the travel time to and from, I expect to see him and that fearsome horse of his any moment. He's sure to hasten his journey for my sake. He dotes on me." A grin of contentment spread across her weathered cheeks. "I was like a mother to him, poor dear, after his own mother died so young."

Tess did not remind her that she'd calculated his arrival just yesterday with as much conviction. "Shoo, you big lump." Tess waved away one of the dogs to pull out a chair next to Lady Stadwell. The lazy hound stood reluctantly, moved two steps and plopped back down with a quiet groan. As she buttered a biscuit for herself, Tess realized that her hands were trembling again. Merely talking about the man unsettled her. She brought the hard biscuit to her mouth then realized her appetite had flown. What was the matter with her? The men she had become acquainted with during her short London season had never made her skittish. But back then, when her father was still alive, she did not need to hide under layers of a wretched disguise. It was as if the wig and brows suffocated all of her confidence and character.

Unable to eat or sit still, Tess pushed up from the table. "The tea!" She hurried to the sideboard. "Would you like some sugar in your tea?" Tess picked up the teapot and poured a cup. She placed it on the table in front of Lady Stadwell.

"Actually, I wouldn't mind having some tea in my tea." Lady Stadwell stared into her cup then looked up at Tess. "This is a cup of hot water."

"I'm so sorry." Tess retrieved the cup and the hot water sloshed onto her thumb. Perhaps Lady Stadwell's china was not so safe after all. Tess scooped some tealeaves from the caddy and poured the hot water from the pot over the infuser. She poured herself a cup as well, hoping it would settle her stomach.

Lady Stadwell patted the seat of the chair next to her. "Come sit, Hortensia. You seem distracted."

"Not at all." Tess sat back down. "You were talking about how you were a mother to Lord Marcliffe. How old was he when his mother died?" As flustered as the subject made her, Tess found herself wanting to hear about him. Maybe something in his past would erase the dashing image she'd formed in her mind.

"He was only a lad of eight. The boy sat up with my poor sister-in-law all night as she labored for her last breaths. My brother found Tallon in the morning, tucked in beside his mother. She had passed on during the night. Naturally, I took it upon myself to be the maternal figure in his life." Lady Stadwell tugged at a lock of her gray hair. "I can tell you I owe most of these white hairs to my nephew. Rarely a summer would pass that we did not have an urgent need for the physician. A displaced shoulder, broken bones, bleeding wounds—it's a wonder my nerves survived it all."

Tess laughed. "It's a wonder Lord Marcliffe survived it all. Perhaps he would have benefited from some discipline."

"Nonsense," Lady Stadwell said abruptly then softened her tone. "One does not tame a wild heart. An authoritarian upbringing makes a boy compliant and weak. The world has more than its share of cowardly men. Men like Lord Marcliffe are a rarity. It would be a spectacular woman indeed to capture his heart."

If only Lord Marcliffe had been one of those weak, cowardly men, Tess thought. Then surely she would not be acting like such a dolt at the mere mention of his return. "But I thought there was a woman in his life already. I'm sure you mentioned her the other evening at dinner." Tess knew very well they'd discussed his mistress. She'd been brimming with curiosity ever since.

"Miss Sparkes? I assure you there is far more attachment on her side than his. I know my nephew too well. She is a diversion. His bedmate, nothing more." Lady Stadwell winked over her cup at Tess.

Tess choked on her tea at Lady Stadwell's bluntness.

Lady Stadwell delivered a hard thump to her back. "You mustn't gulp so."

The pounding of hooves jolted the two dogs from their sleep. "That's him!" Lady Stadwell nearly shrieked the words. She hurried to the window. "I was right. He has returned."

Tess gripped the tasseled edge of the tablecloth. She could not move, but wanted more than anything to run and hide. Damn him for coming to this house. She'd begun to accept her quiet, reclusive existence. And while it was not the same as being with her father, she enjoyed Lady Stadwell's company and had convinced herself she was content. Now every inch of her was alive with raw feelings. Most surprisingly, the arrival of Lady Stadwell's nephew had reinforced her hatred for Sloan. For Sloan was the reason she was destined to be a spinster.

"My word!" Lady Stadwell pressed her hand to her chest.

Tess released her hold on the tablecloth and stood on wobbly legs. "What is it?" She peered at the drive over Lady Stadwell's shoulder. The stallion stood straight up on its back legs. Lord Marcliffe, still in the saddle, waved the stable boy out of the way. Tess released the breath she was holding when the beast finally landed on all fours. Lord Marcliffe swung his leg over the saddle and dropped to the ground.

Lady Stadwell turned to her. "You must put a plate of food together for him at once. He will be starved after such a long ride."

"I was on my way to the garden," Tess sputtered. "But I will serve him before I go."

Lady Stadwell eyed her suspiciously. "Do you not care for Lord Marcliffe?'

Tess hadn't realized she'd been frowning. "Why, I hardly know him. It would be difficult to form an opinion of someone

36

I've only just met." The truth was, she was amazed at how strong an opinion she'd already formed of Lord Marcliffe. "He seems a very fine man."

Lady Stadwell sat back down at the table and unfolded her napkin. "Then please sit and finish breakfast with us. The garden can wait. Haven't the weeds all been plucked?"

"Seems if you yank one, then two will grow in its place," Tess responded with a smile. She walked to the sideboard and spooned eggs and oatmeal pudding onto a plate and topped the whole thing off with a slice of ham. She set the plate down and slinked back to her seat. "I ought to see to brewing some coffee for him. I know he prefers it to tea."

"He'll make do with tea, dear."

Staring down at the biscuit on her plate, Tess nervously began fingering the table covering again. When the click of boot heels sounded in the entry hall, Tess neatly tore off one of the decorative tassels. She tucked it into her pocket and steadied her hands in her lap.

Lady Stadwell glanced casually toward the doorway. "Back so soon, Nephew?"

He filled the entrance. Tess peered up through her powdered lashes. Although he was dressed mostly in black, his presence made the shadowy dining room with its faded blue walls vibrate with light.

He strolled to his aunt and bent down to kiss her on the head. She patted the hand he had placed on her shoulder. "Here I was convinced that you'd be watching for me." He sat directly across from his aunt where Tess had placed the plate.

"As if I don't have better things to do than waste my time waiting for the unpredictable Lord Marcliffe. By the way, why do you not have that beast castrated? He is truly a menace. I have never seen such an ill-behaved animal."

He leaned forward slightly. "Ahh, so you *were* watching out the window for me."

Tess swallowed back a laugh. He caught her mirth and smiled in return.

Lady Stadwell waved her hand. "Such conceit. But if it satisfies you to think that I was anxious for your return then imagine what you will. And you did not answer me. That horse will surely be the death of you."

"I do not have Dante castrated because there is no horse in England to match his speed and stamina. Once they have been cut, they are content to be fat and slow. Nothing slows Dante down." He reached back and winced as he rubbed a shoulder. There was a tear in his coat. "Not even jutting tree branches, unfortunately."

"Good heavens, do you need a physician?" Lady Stadwell asked.

"Not at all." He rotated his shoulder. "Everything still appears to be attached." Lord Marcliffe grabbed a fork and scrambled his oatmeal pudding around on his plate. "Mind you I had the man out to castrate Dante when just a colt. He took one look at the horse and turned around. Told me he'd rather take the knife to himself than get near that animal. After that, I gave up the thought completely."

"Must you always discuss such vulgar topics at table?" Lady Stadwell admonished.

"I believe that you brought it up." He added some salt to the bland food before taking another bite.

"You know, Hortensia, I have a craving for some of your delectable pastries. Why don't you see about getting some ingredients and do some baking for our guest," Lady Stadwell suggested. "Cook has the afternoon off, so you will have the entire kitchen to yourself."

38

Tess was flustered that the attention had suddenly shifted to her. To mask her discomfort, she took a sip of tea and made a rather loud slurping sound in her haste. Lowering the cup, she nodded her agreement.

"You have not said one word, Miss Calloway. So you are a baker? And how did you acquire that skill?" The thin threads of suspicion wove through Lord Marcliffe's words.

She could not fault him for being distrustful since she stammered and blushed at every turn. "I'm self taught. My father's farm had a wonderful kitchen, and I spent many hours there experimenting." Tess was pleased that she had found her tongue again, and her hands began to relax.

"And where exactly was your father's farm located?"

"Why England of course."

He was momentarily silenced by her impudent retort. He leaned back in his chair and studied her. "Quite a secretive chit, I must say."

Tess smiled and placed her napkin on the table. "You seem to believe there is some intriguing story about my past. I assure you there is nothing extraordinary about it. I'm just a country girl orphaned at an early age. If you'll both excuse me." She stood and curtsied to Lady Stadwell and then to Lord Marcliffe. She did not look directly at the latter, but she was certain his dark blue gaze was riveted on her.

ജ

Tess headed to the kitchen. Normally she would have loved the idea of having the kitchen to herself to spend the day baking, but she did not know if she had the mind to enjoy the task today. Lord Marcliffe was back and quite possibly for a lengthy stay. Lady Stadwell was determined to put in motion her plan to snare Sloan. The more Tess thought about the scheme, the more she felt entitled to be a part of it. If it had not been for Sloan's greed, she would be standing in her own warm kitchen chatting and laughing with her father. Instead, she stood in a stranger's kitchen feeling like the ugliest of all the stepsisters and breathless about a man whom she could never have.

The kitchen was dark and still. The heavy, scarred table in the center held a bowl of withered apples and the fire under the kettle had petered out. Tess lit some lamps and carried the sugar and flour sacks from the cupboard. She checked the butter crock. It was empty. She would make a trip up the road to the Hathaways'. They always had plenty of freshly churned butter for purchase.

The side door to the kitchen flung open and smacked the wall. Cook had returned early, Tess thought. She gasped as a hulking, bald-headed man backed through the doorway dragging something heavy. He had to turn his shoulders to squeeze through the passage.

Tess grabbed an iron skillet. "Do not take one more step, thief. I warn you, I am armed!"

The man froze and looked over his shoulder at her. "Aye, that you are." He released his hold on the large makeshift sack he was hauling and stretched up to his full height, bumping his head hard on the top of the lintel. "Hell," he muttered and rubbed his smooth, pink head while he turned slowly to face her. "That's going to be a pretty lump." He held up his meaty slabs of hands. "If I were a thief, would I be bringing things *in* to the house?"

Tess raised the pan higher, knowing how ridiculous she must look trying to ward off a giant with a frying pan. "Well, perhaps you are a particularly dim-witted thief."

He roared with laughter. Tess was sure she saw the pots hanging along the wall vibrate with the sound of it.

"My God, Cyrus, I can't even send you to do a simple task." Lord Marcliffe was suddenly standing directly behind her.

The intruder nodded toward Tess. "You didn't say nothing 'bout wenches armed with pots."

"You can lower your weapon, Miss Calloway. Cyrus only looks like an ogre." Lord Marcliffe removed his coat as he strolled past her. He grabbed hold of what looked to be a side of mutton wrapped in paper, part of the load Cyrus had bundled in a vast oilcloth. "Christ, did she do that to you?" Lord Marcliffe rose to his toes to get a closer look at the bump on the man's head.

"No. It was the doorway. The house was built for elves."

Lord Marcliffe shook his head. "One would think you woke up just this morning as tall as a forest pine. Learn to duck, you towering fool. Now help me with the goods." There was a sparkle in his eyes as he shot a glance at Tess. "Miss Calloway, if you would be so kind as to make room in the larder for these things."

Cyrus nodded cautiously at Tess then walked a wide circle around her with heavy sacks of potatoes and onions slung over his shoulders.

"You have apparently made quite an impression on my friend," Lord Marcliffe said. "I've seen him take on six armed Frenchmen and leave them all in a crumpled heap, but one small woman with a skillet, and just look at him tiptoeing around."

Tess pushed aside the scant items on the larder shelves, and Lord Marcliffe hefted the meat atop the cooling stone slab. "Cyrus will be staying on for awhile. Thus the need to stock the

41

larder."

Tess knew full well that Lord Marcliffe was using that as an excuse to help his aunt. Lady Stadwell was correct. Her nephew did dote on her. And now she could add generosity to the list of appealing traits possessed by Lord Marcliffe. Surely he could list as many unappealing traits about Hortensia Calloway.

When Lord Marcliffe retrieved his coat Tess noticed for the first time that his white shirt was stained with blood. It had clearly been more than a scratch he'd suffered on the road.

"Christ, Marcliffe, what happened to your shoulder?" Cyrus asked.

"Tree branch came out of nowhere."

"Learn to duck." Cyrus seemed pleased with his retort. "Your lordship," he added quickly.

"This witty gentleman, Miss Calloway, served as my sergeant. I don't think I'd ever step on a battlefield without this titan beside me. Cyrus, this is Miss Calloway, my aunt's new companion."

To Lady Stadwell's other visitors she was a nonentity. She had faded into the wallpaper just as Beadle had hoped. But Lord Marcliffe was different. He treated her as if she existed, even introducing her to his army mate. A lump formed in her throat. She hadn't realized how much she'd missed being spoken to as if she was someone worth speaking to.

Her face must have betrayed her thoughts because he offered a heartening smile. "I assure you Cyrus is harmless," he said, misreading her emotions. He adjusted his cravat. "I am anxious to taste some of your pastries. My aunt says that you put London's bakers to shame."

"I'm afraid Lady Stadwell is exaggerating my skills. But I shall try not to disappoint either of you." She nodded to his friend. "And I will try not to swing kitchen utensils at your visitor." Tess was thankful that Lord Marcliffe had neglected to supply butter. The house was suddenly becoming crowded with overlarge men, and she could think of nothing more inviting than a long walk alone. "I'm off to the Hathaways' for butter." She took a basket from a hook.

"I might join you." He kneaded his thigh with his knuckles. "I always get stiff after a long ride and a stroll will do me some good."

"Really, you mustn't... I mean I would rather... I don't mind going alone."

Lord Marcliffe stared at her. "I hardly know what to think of that response. Either you have some secret rendezvous planned or you find my company thoroughly disagreeable."

"I think it is the latter," Cyrus interjected.

Lord Marcliffe raised an eyebrow at his friend who shrugged in response.

"Mr. Cyrus, I'm afraid Lord Marcliffe has decided that I am leading a double life."

"I believe nothing of the sort, Miss Calloway." His tone was serious. "I am, however, very protective of my aunt."

"Then you can believe me when I say that I have grown extremely fond of Lady Stadwell and I would never do anything to compromise her trust."

He considered her for an uncomfortably long moment, hoping, it seemed, to gauge the truth of her words.

Cyrus cleared his throat. "I'll be heading out to unhook the wagon. Sorry if I caused you any fright, miss." He stopped just short of smacking his head on the doorway again. With excess caution, he crouched comically low as he exited.

Tess curtsied and slipped by Lord Marcliffe to follow Cyrus out the side door.

"Miss Calloway," he called before she could make a clean escape.

A lock of his silken black hair had fallen across his forehead and her fingers itched to smooth it back. "Thank you for taking such good care of my aunt. She is very fond of you and she has not trusted anyone since—" He stepped closer.

Tess retreated toward the open doorway. He stopped, seeming to understand that she did not want him to come any closer. His gaze was riveted on her mouth.

"I apologize if I cause you unease."

"'Tis a nervous twitch, my lord." She caught her trembling bottom lip with her teeth and turned away to head into the gray morning.

Chapter Four

The walk brought clarity to Tess's thoughts. Her fingers stiffening, she shifted the basket to the other hand. She was no longer thinking as charitably about Lady Stadwell's nephew. The blackguard had known exactly what he was doing when he'd strutted his breath-stealing, naked form across the floor of his bedchamber. *Give the poor, pathetic chit a thrill. She'll never be this close to an unclothed man again.* A tingle ran up Tess's spine as she imagined tracing the thin line of black hair that trailed down his abdomen.

She made an effort to concentrate on the recipes she'd be preparing. She thought of butter browning and nearly melted at the idea of touching his golden skin. How would she manage not to make a complete fool of herself with her spinsterish disguise and newfound desire? The answer, she determined, was to make herself scarce whenever he was about.

By late afternoon, the sky outside had darkened with heavy clouds. Tess lit the kitchen lamp and moved on to her next recipe. She stirred plump currants, nutmeg, cinnamon and butter. Lord Marcliffe had filled the pantry well.

She painstakingly decorated the cooled marzipan-iced cakes with almond slivers and candied ginger. Her confidence returned as she marveled at her creations. The crusts on her apple and clove pies were some of the prettiest she'd ever made.

She was beginning to feel at ease again. She set the kettle to boil for tea.

Lady Stadwell's dogs bounded into the kitchen, bringing with them the pungent smells of the barn. "Out!" Tess herded them through the door and nearly fell over the man she was intent on avoiding. The rolled shirtsleeves and the hay clinging to his trousers left no doubt that he had been fixing the damage his stallion had caused.

At the water pump, he scrubbed his hands and face with water. As he bent over, she couldn't help noticing that his shirt clung to his broad back with sweat. An earl had no business doing labor and, more importantly, no business looking so damned good doing it. It was all done on purpose, she thought, and then cringed at her own vanity. As if Lord Marcliffe cared at all what impression he made on homely Hortensia.

He straightened and raked wet lines into his hair with his damp fingers. "Miss Calloway, there is a mouthwatering aroma coming from the kitchen. You've been busy it seems."

"I have and I best return to it. There is still much to do."

Please don't follow, she silently wished as she stepped back into the kitchen. As usual, her wishes produced the opposite effect. Lord Marcliffe stomped the caked dirt from his boots before stepping inside. Without being asked, she ladled ale from the barrel into a tankard and set it on the counter beside him.

He saluted her with the tankard. "You've anticipated my needs, Miss Calloway."

Tess tried not to focus on the strong muscles of his throat as he swallowed, quenching his thirst. But one particular trickle of sweat held her attention as it slipped into the hollow at the base of his throat.

He moved to the large trestle table and began shoveling her handmade cakes into his hungry mouth as if they were grapes off a vine.

Tess could only stare. All her hard work and he could have been eating stale bread for all he could taste in his haste to devour the pastries.

For a moment, he stopped his chewing and glanced at her. The wide-eyed expression he flashed her resembled that of a delinquent caught with his thumb in the pie. There were several crumbs clinging to the dark stubble of his chin. Tess stepped forward and used her thumb to wipe the crumbs away. The roughness of his beard matched his rugged appearance.

"You've got something on your face," she said. They stood so close that Tess could have counted his lashes, except they were far too numerous. Her lips curled. Beadle be damned. Right now, under the faded wig and powdered lashes, she needed the confidence that her smile had always brought her. A dour, grumpy expression was not a necessity for the disguise. She smiled brightly, and he blinked as if momentarily dazzled.

Tess walked back to the other side of the table, leaving him speechless. She was going to prove to herself that she could handle this man, no matter what tricks he had up his sleeve. And that was when a notion popped into her head. Or rather, it seemed, the idea had been planted days ago and had only now sprouted. She would ensnare Sloan herself. *She* would become the temptress that Lady Stadwell hoped to conjure to bring the villain to justice.

"More ale, my lord?"

"Tea would be better." Having regained his tongue, the earl surveyed the spread of pastries with an eager eye. "What's inside these round ones?" Without waiting for a response he picked up a saffron cookie and shoved it into his mouth.

"I hardly imagine that the ingredients matter. At that speed, your tongue does not actually have time to taste them."

Scottie Barrett

He shrugged. "As long as there's sugar inside, that's all I need."

Tess watched half-annoyed and half-charmed as four hours of hard work disappeared. She surveyed the shrinking rows of finished pastries and laughed. "Perhaps I should have doubled the recipes. I do hope you will leave some for your aunt."

He arched one of his finely formed brows and shot her a mock glare across the table. Piling a cookie on top of a marzipan cake, he lifted the double-layered treat into the air like he was toasting with a glass of brandy. Lowering the pastries to his mouth, he took a delicate bite and chewed it slowly.

"That is not exactly what I meant by doubling it, but as long as you are enjoying them." The kettle whistled, and Tess reached for it. By the time she'd poured the hot water, the man had pushed the layered dessert into his mouth.

A mischievous smile erupted behind the barrage of crumbs that tumbled from his mouth.

With a shake of her head, Tess pushed the cup of tea toward him.

"Sorry," he said. "I couldn't resist."

Well at least there might be one thing about her he found hard to resist.

"Miss Calloway, I need you to do me a favor. Please come up with some diversion to take my aunt's mind off this scheme of hers. Maybe a major needlework project. Something that would occupy her and let her forget these absurd plans of revenge."

"You think because Lady Stadwell is a woman, something as frivolous as embroidery will peel her mind from the need to bring justice to a swindler? A swindler who has crushed her heart? A swindler who has ruined her financially?" She set the
48

kettle down with a clang atop the stove. "You are not the man I thought you were. How could you have such a ridiculous opinion of your aunt?"

She had not meant to speak so abruptly, but she knew how much Lady Stadwell had suffered and her pain was equal.

Lord Marcliffe stepped closer. "Miss Calloway, I only mean to save my aunt more heartache."

Fearing she would say something else which might put her position in jeopardy, she reached for one of the sweets and pushed the entire miniature cake into her mouth. Instantly, she breathed in a stray crumb and began coughing and sputtering. Her hand flew over her mouth before she sprayed him with bits of pastry.

He folded her free hand around his tankard, and she took a drink.

"Thank you," she said as her coughing subsided. She set the vessel down and brushed the crumbs from her bodice. "I daresay that was a ladylike display."

He laughed. "Remind me to teach you how to shovel a pastry properly without causing harm to yourself." His gaze was unnerving. "I hope you will reconsider and convince my aunt that she must put an end to this foolish idea."

Tess returned to her task. "Not only do I think Lady Stadwell's plan important and clever, but I intend to help her with it if she needs my assistance." She plopped the filling into the tart shells in a sloppy fashion contradictory to her usual style. Lamplight cast his tall, wavering shadow across her flouring board.

"Perhaps you could be the one to woo Sloan and make him confess all his darkest secrets."

A tiny whimper escaped her lips. Her heart felt as if it were being squeezed. The man was a stranger, how could his ridiculing words injure her so?

"I apologize, Miss Calloway." His voice had lowered to a near whisper. "I forget myself. Those words came out completely wrong."

The sound of pity in his voice made her want to flee the manor for good and all.

"It is only that there is much danger when a man like Sloan is involved. Far more danger than you can imagine. He has led some men to their death."

"I'm well aware of the dangers."

"And how is that?" he asked.

Tess pressed her hands on the board to keep them from trembling. "I know only what your aunt has told me and I want to help her. Now I would like to finish these tarts before the crusts grow soggy."

She tensed. What prying questions would he ask next? How would she keep from blurting out her own tale of terror in regards to Sloan?

But the questions didn't come. Lord Marcliffe collected a handful of cakes. "Extraordinary pastries," he said before leaving.

৪১

Tallon braced one hand on either side of the library window and stared out at the grounds. At one time the boxwoods had been so lush and precisely trimmed that from the house they looked like a straight, solid wall of green. Now they were sparse like lattice, barely resembling a hedge. It saddened him to see the gardens he'd spent so much time in as a child fall into such a state of disrepair. His aunt had good reason to be plagued with thoughts of revenge. Tallon tightened his fists as he thought about Sloan. The bloody bastard left a trail of despair and heartbreak wherever he went and he thoroughly deserved to meet up with a bitter end. But using an innocent woman to discover his deceitful schemes was dishonorable.

The solitary black-garbed figure drew Tallon from his thoughts. Hortensia struggled with a small gardening cart across the uneven lawn. Her oversized skirts caught on her heels twice and she had to stop to pull the hem out from under her boot. The cart toppled to one side as she reached the scraggy path of boxwoods. Garden tools and pots of flowers spilled to the ground.

One of the stable cats raced by the fallen cart with a bird in its mouth. From the window he could hear Hortensia call to the animal. At once she snatched up her heavy skirts and ran after the little hunter. Tallon watched in amazement as she flew gracefully across the yard. How was it possible for her to be so clumsy one minute and so agile the next? In the kitchen she could barely fix a cup of tea without shattering the porcelain, yet she had created complex pastries like an artisan. He had to confess that he took some satisfaction in the fact that his nearness disconcerted her. Truth was, she unsettled him, as well. When she'd wiped the cookie crumbs from his face and backed up the bold gesture with a smile, he'd found his usual state of composure compromised. She was so bland in color, hair and style, but when her mouth opened into a smile it was as blinding as if someone had peeled the plain brown wrapping off a gem both rare and brilliant.

The cat plopped into the tall grass, teeth still clamped on its twittering prey. Hortensia stomped toward it and firmly grabbed it by the scruff of the neck. She forced open the tiny jaw and the bird fluttered off spraying feathers as it headed for the safety of the nearest tree. The cat slumped off in anger.

Tallon laughed aloud and headed outside. He had no particular reason for leaving the house except the activity taking place on the lawn suddenly seemed far more entertaining than the dreary confines of the library. And strangely enough he found himself drawn to her company, the queer, little misfit with the breathtaking smile. And though it was obvious she was hiding something about her past, he was convinced she meant no harm to his aunt.

Tallon reached the overturned cart as Hortensia retrieved her fallen pots. "I believe you've injured that cat's pride. It may never hunt again."

The girl startled and dropped the yellow daisy she'd just picked up. "Good. The little savage. That's the third sparrow he's stuck his teeth into this week. The other two were not as lucky."

He stooped to pick up the small shovel and placed it on the righted cart. "Don't you know it's wrong to interfere with nature?"

"Nature, indeed. God gives one animal claws, fangs and a vicious thirst for blood while the other animal has nothing but a sweet song. 'Tis hardly fair." Hortensia kept her face down as she spoke. She organized her cart in neat rows with trembling fingers.

"What animal wouldn't give up claws and fangs for a pair of wings?" Tallon handed her the straw hat that had flown from her head as she dashed after the cat.

She planted the hat on her head and secured the ribbons under her chin. "What good are wings when your enemy has the stealth and cunning of a practiced murderer?"

"Are you certain you're still talking about the cat? By your tone, one would think that I, too, had walked out here with a bird clenched between my teeth."

She fiddled with the items in her cart. "My heavens, I sound like a harpy. You'll have to excuse me, Lord Marcliffe, sometimes my emotions get the best of me. Thank you for your help." Again her bulky clothes hampered her movement as she pushed the unwieldy cart across the yard.

"I imagine that little bird is thankful for your strong emotions." He could see the corner of her mouth turn up and had the sudden urge to see her radiant smile again. It did not appear often enough, and he was determined to change that.

The girl was hurting deep inside, and Tallon had more than a suspicion that Sloan was the cause. Hortensia was too in favor of his aunt's plan. Yesterday she'd all but volunteered to play a key role in the outlandish scheme. As if Sloan could ever appreciate the woman beneath the bland exterior, the spirit that refused to be smothered by heavy mourning garb. Was it possible he was finding this girl appealing despite her drab appearance?

He caught up with her in two strides. "I believe you would have an easier time of it if you weren't always clad in so many layers of oversized skirts." He gently brushed her hands aside and took the handles of the cart.

She stepped aside. "I need it over there along the wall, where the shade is greatest. We are not all free-spirits, my lord, where we feel comfortable parading around in the nude."

"I wasn't suggesting you remove all your clothes. Just the first four layers." He'd only meant to shock the brazen chit for bursting into his chambers uninvited and waking him from an alcohol-steeped sleep. It had been an unkind thing to do to a sheltered girl, and he was thoroughly ashamed of himself. And it pained him to think that his monstrous scars, almost more than his nakedness, had shaken the girl.

Tallon pushed the cart toward the moss-covered stone wall.

A lizard darted into a deep crevice. "Don't plants prefer the light?"

Hortensia laughed. "These seedlings are digitalis. They would die in the sun. They much prefer a cool shady spot."

"Digitalis? You sound as if you've done some reading on horticulture."

"I've been known to pick up a book or two."

Tallon adjusted the cart so that it remained steady on the uneven ground. "I did not mean to imply that you were without curiosity. On the contrary, you seem to know a lot about many things." He was rambling on like a school lad.

With a puff of skirts, Hortensia dropped onto her knees and began digging a hole in the moist earth. She sighed softly, and Tallon enjoyed the sound of it.

"My father and I would garden together." The words seemed to catch in her throat. She picked up the small pot beside her and slid the seedling gently onto her palm before tucking it into the hole. "I'm sure you must have more interesting things to tend to this morning than watching me."

"If you would like me to leave, you need only say it." Though she had said it, hadn't she? Had he misread her reactions to him? Perhaps she was nervous around him because she wished to be rid of him. "I'm sorry if my presence disturbs you. And I'm sorry about your father. Was it a long illness?"

She shook her head and hastily dug three more holes, then slid a fragile seedling from its pot into her hand. "You may stay if you wish, but I'm sure you will find this awfully dull."

"With such a heartfelt invitation to stay," he quipped, "how can I possibly depart? I'll make myself useful." He picked up the small trowel. "Show me what to do." He crouched beside her.

Hortensia froze for a moment then glanced at him from beneath the wide brim of her hat. Then without warning, she smiled. He rocked back on his heels, landing himself on his arse. Although it was not the source of his embarrassment, he rubbed his bad leg. "It's always giving me a problem, you know."

She reached out a dirt-covered hand. "Perhaps you need some help righting yourself—" her green eyes looked pointedly at his leg, "—what with your bothersome injury." She quirked her lip, but fortunately for him, it did not erupt into a full smile. It was a weapon she obviously knew she possessed and she seemed to know exactly when to use it.

Although there was something very tempting about taking hold of her petite hand, he decided to save an ounce of his dignity and clambered to his feet without her assistance.

He hunkered down on his haunches again and twisted the trowel in the soil, making clumsy work of it and sending dirt flying. She swept the soil from her dress. "Generally, I try to keep all of the ground down here for the plants."

Tallon laughed. What a complete imbecile he was being and every one of her reactions was charming. "Obviously, my farming skills are lacking."

"Be sure to dig a hole that is wider and deeper than the pot the plant is in now. This will give the roots plenty of chance to spread." She demonstrated with her own trowel.

Tallon set to the task. "You know a great deal about many things, Miss Calloway. I am surprised."

"Oh, and why might that be, my lord?"

"It is just that you seem so young to have already learned so much." He glanced at her. Only her cheek was visible from under the brim of the hat. It flushed pink with his compliment.

"I am rarely idle. Even though my years are few, I have had

55

many experiences."

Tallon picked up a pot. She reached over and stopped him from yanking out the seedling. Her hand was cool and slightly callused, yet it warmed his skin.

"You must invite the tiny plant out. It is a shock for it to be leaving its cozy home. If you are too rough, it will wither away in its new place." She picked up his free hand and placed it under the seedling. "Give the pot a small shake." She moved her hand with his. The plant slid slowly into his waiting palm. She pulled her hands away, and he felt the same disappointment that struck him when she made it clear that she did not crave his company.

Leaning over, he gently tucked the tiny green stem into its hole and packed the soil around it. He smiled. "I think I did that rather well."

She stopped her digging and stared at his work. "Not bad at all." She never looked at him. He could see only the ends of her turned up mouth, but her devastating smile had already become etched permanently in his mind.

Chapter Five

The trail of smoke from the chimney was Tess's compass across the meadow. Her thin bonnet provided little protection against the late afternoon chill. She climbed over the low stone wall, her basket overflowing with wild asters and bluebells. Unfamiliar carriages lined the drive and for a moment Tess was convinced she'd taken the wrong path, yet the familiar brick manor loomed.

To her surprise, she found Lady Stadwell alone in the parlor.

"Is Lord Marcliffe entertaining?" Tess asked.

"I'm afraid my nephew will have little time to pay us any attention this evening."

Tess blushed. Had her interest in Lord Marcliffe been so pathetically obvious?

"He's attending to some business." Lady Stadwell offered her a sympathetic smile. Her towering pile of curls, some real, most fake, had tilted and she swatted ineffectually at a lock of hair that had fallen into her eyes.

Carelessly, Tess deposited the wild flowers on the side table. Certain the disappointment was written plain on her face, she turned her back on her employer and jammed the stems into a vase.

"That's if you consider interviewing a flock of powdered, perfumed women business." Lady Stadwell's conspiratorial whisper seemed louder to Tess's ears than normal speech. "The stubborn boy has finally taken my advice." Lady Stadwell's elbow slipped off the chair's arm and she sloshed cognac into her lap.

Normally Tess would have rushed to mop it up. Instead, without a word, she fled the room. Her cape hung heavy on her neck as she raced down the hall to the library. Thankfully, the door was unlocked. She pushed it open and tripped over the threshold, landing on her hands and knees amid a sea of skirts.

Lord Marcliffe shot out from behind the desk. "Hortensia, what the devil?"

She refused his offered hand and got to her feet. "I would like to be considered for the position."

His expression could not be misconstrued. His dark lashes lowered, concealing his sympathetic gaze. "I am searching for certain assets."

"Assets?"

"Not the ones you possess, Hortensia." His gaze lifted. He'd apparently found the courage to look at her again. By the way his lips tightened, she was certain he was trying to suppress a smile of pity very much like the one his aunt had given her. Knowing that he found her physically repulsive made her stomach clench. She balled her fists, her fingernails cutting crescents into her palms.

Tess glanced around the room, taking the measure of her competition. There were three women, all quite lovely and all looking at her with varying degrees of amusement and curiosity. Two had applied quite a bit of paint, giving them doll-like appearances. She couldn't help noticing that they were all dark-haired. Was that, she wondered, a particular preference of

Sloan's, or was it Lord Marcliffe who preferred brunettes?

Her fingers flew to her head to smooth the frizzy dark strands. The wig had once been sleek, but now it resembled a ratty horsetail. She had no money to replace it.

The tall woman standing nearest her snickered. "Perhaps, girls, we ought to leave. It seems we have been outshone."

"You have indeed. Now, I suggest you shut up," Lord Marcliffe growled.

The woman blinked hard as though she'd been slapped.

Coming to her rescue did nothing to mend the rip he'd put in her heart a few moments ago. "I am not above begging. I would do anything you ask. *Anything.*"

"Would you go so far as seducing the man?"

Tess found herself unable to reply. She knew it would come as a complete shock to Lord Marcliffe to find that not only would she be willing to seduce Sloan, but she would bed him for the rest of her bloody days if it meant exacting punishment.

"Hortensia, I asked you a question." Lord Marcliffe's voice dropped to a low, nearly inaudible level. A sure sign that he was angry.

"Yes, I suppose, if I must do." Her gaze skittered away from his hard stare and she focused on the rose-patterned wallpaper over his shoulder.

"That's a bloody fine thing to admit."

Her father had been the center of her life, and now he was gone, all because of that loathsome man. She looked up at Lord Marcliffe. "You don't know anything about me. You don't understand what this means to me."

He stared at her for a long time. "Bloody hell." He hitched his hip on the edge of the desk and folded his arms across his chest. "Hortensia, you force me to be cruel. Intelligence, wit and charm are all lost on Sloan. He has only one requisite for the women he takes to bed. Beauty."

The other women in the room laughed.

Tess mimicked him by crossing her arms. "Are we talking about you, my lord, or Mr. Sloan?" Another comment their audience found amusing.

"You three may go," he said, ushering them out with a dismissive sweep of his hand.

"But what about the position?" the tall woman whined.

"Go."

With chins raised as though to preserve their dignity, the women bustled out of the library. Their overpowering perfume lingered once the door was shut.

The expression on Lord Marcliffe's face made Tess feel that perhaps she should have left with the others.

He strode purposefully toward her. She gasped when he took hold of her arms and lifted her up onto her toes. He stared boldly at her lips then lifted his gaze to her eyes. "Do not waste my time any further or you will find yourself without a position entirely. And for Christ's sake, stop looking at me with those unbelievable eyes of yours." He released her. "Go to your room, Hortensia. I've had about enough of my aunt's ridiculous machinations." He turned his back on her.

She could reveal herself to him, but what if he found her wanting? Found her copper-colored hair unfashionable or not to Sloan's taste? If she pushed him too far, she would find herself holed up in her father's frigid townhouse unable to even afford kindling to feed one of the massive hearths.

The stubborn side of her personality asserted itself. "Perhaps you are unnecessary. What is to stop me from seducing him without your help?"

He spun around to face her. She waited for his stinging laughter and instead found herself staring into eyes grown cold and hard.

"My sweet, innocent Hortensia..." His black brows lowered. "It seems I misjudged you. You are no different than the very expensive females I just dismissed."

She felt heat flood her face. Why did he have to say *my*? The word meant nothing to him, certainly. But to her it had a possessive, heart-clutching sound. The fanciful notion of belonging to him had hidden in her heart from the moment she'd met him and had recently swelled to unmanageable proportions. And now it was clear her bold admissions had lost her all of Lord Marcliffe's regard.

She took a few steadying breaths before returning to the parlor. Lady Stadwell, seemingly unaware that any time had elapsed, took up her conversation where she'd left off. Tess registered the name Sloan, but, still reeling from Lord Marcliffe's fury, she only half-listened to the now-familiar refrain of betrayal and death. She peered at her image in the mirror. At this moment, she felt all the ugliness was inside her. Through the fog of despair, she heard Lady Stadwell speak her name.

"Pardon?"

"You needn't fret so about your appearance. Even Marcliffe seems quite fond of you as you are."

Impossible, Tess thought, as she studied her reflection. She furrowed her beetle brows. Lord Marcliffe, fond of her in this trollish incarnation? Absurd. Clearly, the woman was more foxed than she appeared.

Tess peeled Lady Stadwell's fingers from the tumbler of cognac. "Lady Stadwell, I think you've been dreaming. Perhaps a warm dinner and early bedtime will help."

Lord Marcliffe did not come to the dining room for the evening meal. Perhaps he'd followed one of the women home. Or perhaps he couldn't stomach a meal with the pathetic Miss Calloway.

By the time the dishes were cleared it was apparent that her dinner companion needed sleep. The food had not negated the effects of the cognac. Bearing most of Lady Stadwell's weight, Tess navigated the stairs. With some effort, she managed the bedchamber door. Dressing Lady Stadwell in nightclothes proved an even more difficult task.

Once in bed, Lady Stadwell nestled her head contentedly in the mountain of soft pillows. "My eyes are too tired. Could you read to me?" She handed Tess a book from the bed stand.

Not surprisingly, Lady Stadwell drifted off to sleep after one chapter. Tess had read the romantic novel as if she'd been reading a monotonous sermon. She set the book aside. The stress of the day had faded from Lady Stadwell's face. Tess wished she could find that same peace. But even her nights were restless.

The icy water weighing down her skirts and her father's lifeless stare still haunted her dreams.

༄

Tallon could not remember the last time he had ridden so hard. Spurring his horse into a frenzy, he jumped every obstacle they came to in the stark moonlit night. His horse was sleek with sweat, as was he. Yet the air was so cold, his breath was visible.

Frustrated, he slowed the horse to a trot. Even with the insane ride he'd taken, he could not shake Hortensia from his thoughts. He had no idea when or how his possessive feelings for her had begun, but the thought of her with Sloan enraged him.

What was it about this strange and plain little creature that had him in such a lather? His lithe, blonde mistress waited to service his every need, yet he hadn't paid a visit to her since meeting Hortensia. This morning while poring over paperwork his mind had wandered. He'd dreamed of kneeling between Hortensia's thighs and tasting every intimate inch of her. When she flashed that rare but intriguing smile, it took him hours to stop thinking about her lips. And now what was really driving him mad was her obvious obsession with Sloan.

After stabling his horse, Tallon stopped at the water pump. He stuck his head under the icy water, but it did nothing to chill his emotions. He would find out her motives. And he would find out tonight, or he would never sleep.

The door to his aunt's room was ajar. He glanced in and watched in silence as Hortensia, with loving care, tucked another blanket around his aunt. She cupped her hand around the flickering flame of her candle. The dim light illuminated the sadness in her face. She slipped out of the room and softly shut the door behind her. She obviously did not notice him standing in the dark hallway. A little cry escaped her when she stepped on his toes.

He gripped her arms, jostling the candlestick she held. Hot wax dripped onto his shirtsleeve. "Who's Sloan to you?"

She stared up at him. Rivulets of water fell from his drenched hair, soaking his linen shirt and her dress, as well. "Do not dare look at me with those lost kitten eyes. I will know why you seek to prostitute yourself to Sloan."

"I hate you," she said, her voice cracking with emotion. Her trembling caused the candle flame to waver.

He could not believe what a profound effect her declaration

had on him. He swallowed hard. "Fine, we've established how you feel about me, but it does not explain your fascination with that bastard."

Tears spilled down her cheeks, leaving a strange, milky trail as they went. "Fascination? I abhor the man. He took everything from me. He is the reason I have turned myself into this servile creature who must cower at the very voice of her master."

"I have yet to see you cower," he said with a grin as he wiped a tear away with his thumb.

"Perhaps, that is a bit of an exaggeration," she said, and without any warning she smiled.

"A bit," he agreed. "Can I assume your father invested in Sloan's land scheme as did Lord Stadwell? Was Beadle the intermediary?"

"Yes and yes. But Beadle did help me after my father died. He saw to it that he was buried—" She clamped her lips together.

With the heel of her free hand she pushed hard at his chest. When she didn't manage to budge him, she shoved with more force. He gripped the sides of her waist and lowered his face. Her sweet breath whispered across his mouth.

"Enough." He gazed at where his fingers held her. Intrigued, he used both hands to circle her waist. "That's the tiniest waist I've ever had my hands around. Why do you wear these oversized frocks?"

"Because I am modest, Lord Marcliffe."

"How amusing. A modest whore." Still perplexed, he peered down again at his hands bracketing her waist. He rubbed his thumbs in the hollow of her belly. "You are like a mirage. There is something there, and then it is gone. When I think of you I can't quite picture you in my mind." He closed his eyes. "No, I cannot describe you. Why is that, do you think?" He opened his eyes. "And there you are, sweetly familiar."

His head dipped nearer, his lips nearly grazing her mouth. She clutched at his shirt, clearly not realizing the effect she was having on him. Her innocence startled him. She was completely unaware of how badly he wanted to kiss her. The obstacle of the candle infuriated him and he blew it out. The darkness enveloped them.

"I'm desperate to be a part of your plan. I should be allowed the satisfaction of seeing Sloan pay."

He released his hold on her. "I cannot allow it. I will handle everything." He left Hortensia and her pouty but incredibly appealing mouth alone in the dark.

Chapter Six

Tess set up the cribbage board and pegs. She hoped a game of cards would offer a diversion. Dinner had been uncomfortably long and Tess had barely managed to eat a forkful. Lord Marcliffe had sat at the end of the table in sullen silence. Tess was certain she was the source of his grim mood.

A sharp rapping at the door sent the mastiffs skidding across the parlor floor. Their barking soon became grating.

"Excuse me," Tess said to Lady Stadwell as she pushed away from the card table. Irritated, she went to see if someone was getting the door.

Cyrus stood in the open doorway, blocking her view of the visitor. When he stepped aside, Tess was more than shocked to see Beadle enter. It was the first time he'd deigned to call since dropping her on Lady Stadwell's doorstep. Cyrus took Beadle's hat and coat and tossed them over the umbrella stand. Beadle's expression soured at the big man's rudeness.

Cyrus motioned with his head. "Lord Marcliffe is waiting for you in the library."

There was only a flicker of acknowledgement as Beadle glanced at Tess before his expression went blank. "Miss Calloway, I do hope you are finding your employment satisfactory."

Not waiting for a response, he walked officiously in the direction of the library. Beadle was persisting with the ruse using the fake name he'd supplied her. Tess supposed he wanted to continue an amiable business relationship with Lady Stadwell. She would not take kindly to having been tricked into sheltering an orphan whose father had died ignominiously.

What business could Lord Marcliffe have with Beadle? What if the meeting had something to do with Lord Marcliffe's pointed questioning of her last week? Perhaps she was being too cynical. It was entirely possible that Beadle had solved her financial dilemma. All she could do now was go back to the game and wait. She would know soon enough why he had come.

Lady Stadwell had already dealt the cards and she'd poured each of them a generous serving of sherry. Her cheeks had a rosy flush, and Tess suspected that this was not her first drink. Tess wondered if she'd consumed as much sherry before Sloan. "A glass of spirits always makes the game a tad more amusing." She took a sip. "I find if I have enough, I am pleased whether I win or lose."

They refilled their glasses at the start of each round. Cribbage was never one of Tess's favorite games, but sherry certainly made the time pass quickly.

બુ

A heavy hand nudged Tess awake. She lifted her head off the table to peer up at Cyrus. He smiled and plucked off the playing card plastered to her forehead. The fire in the hearth was now a pile of glowing coals. The big man leaned over a dozing Lady Stadwell and scooped her easily into his arms. Tess got to her feet and followed behind. At the landing, she grabbed a handful of Cyrus's coat and let him guide her up the stairs.

Even with her mind bleary from drink, she instantly recalled Beadle's visit. Surely he'd gone by now. The nerve of the man to not have spoken with her. "Did Mr. Beadle leave a message for me?" she asked Cyrus.

"Mr. Beadle is still with Lord Marcliffe."

She miscalculated a step and her toe smacked the edge of the stair. Had she had not been gripping the coat of the very solid giant in front of her, she would have fallen. If the meeting was taking this long, then certainly she could not be the topic of their conversation.

Tess tucked Lady Stadwell in as best she could then tottered off to her room. After struggling into her nightclothes, she tore off her unbearably itchy wig and shoved her hair under the sleeping cap.

She had started to drift off to sleep again when the dogs began another tiresome round of barking. Fighting dizziness, she swung her legs over the side of the mattress and gripped the bedpost. Her head throbbed. *Blasted sherry.* She would pay for her indulgence in the morning. Trying not to jostle her head, she treaded ever so gently into the hallway. She gripped the banister for support as she peered over the railing.

"What is the commotion?" she called down to Lord Marcliffe who stood at the base of the staircase with Beadle. She narrowed her eyes. The light from the wall sconces was entering her already pounding brain.

She was instructed by both men, speaking in near unison, to put something on and come downstairs. It was silly, really. The nightgown that Lady Stadwell had been nice enough to provide her was as revealing as a sack.

She staggered back to her room and pulled the ancient black dress over the thick flannel shift, feeling like she had two possessive husbands awaiting her. With luck, Beadle had brought her good news. Perhaps her days in this dreadful disguise were coming to an end. She took a quick glance in the small looking glass that she usually avoided. Her eyebrows were still in place and, except for the small spot where the card had adhered to her forehead, her skin was still powdered. But it had caked in spots, and she smoothed it to give herself a more natural appearance.

The alcohol made her unsteady. She carefully planted both feet on each step before proceeding to the next.

"You are as drunk as a piper, Miss Calloway," Lord Marcliffe said.

She ignored him and turned her attention to the other man. "Mr. Beadle." She said his name in a breathy, anticipatory whisper. He was, after all, the man who held her future.

Lord Marcliffe muttered a curse under his breath. She ignored that, too.

"Can I come out of exile? Have you managed to sell the townhouse?"

"Rumor is, your hero bid it in a game of Faro. And lost," Lord Marcliffe said between gritted teeth.

A wave of nausea threatened to overcome her. "Mr. Beadle, please tell me that isn't true," she pleaded.

Beadle shrugged. "I only wanted to see you better situated."

"If you hadn't been such a damn fool and wagered the resources, you could have easily cleared her father's debts and kept her safe from Fleet. Admit it, you whoreson, you scared her into hiding and then absconded with the scant remainder of her inheritance."

Tess wobbled unsteadily on the step above the landing. And here she'd thought her life had sunk to the bottom. Apparently she had farther to fall. Beadle shot Lord Marcliffe a vicious look and moved forward, taking her hands in his. "Do not worry, my dear Hortensia, you will come home with me. I will take care of you." He moved closer, his voice dropping to a hoarse whisper. "I cannot promise marriage, of course, as I'd hoped."

Life with Beadle. Wouldn't that be a splendid end to an already wretched situation? "Mr. Beadle, I don't understand how my father ever came to trust you. Your craving for gambling obviously trumps your honor."

"Damn it, Beadle," Lord Marcliffe said, and hauled him away by the scruff of his neck.

Beadle's sudden release of her hands unbalanced her. She keeled forward. How Lord Marcliffe managed it, she had no idea, but he insinuated himself between them, and she toppled neatly into his arms. Her face pressed against his chest. There was something so warm and comforting about being in his embrace that the tears came in a torrent, soaking his lapels.

When she pulled her face away, she noticed that she'd left the pale dusting that hid her lashes on the brushed velvet of his lapels. She swiped ineffectively at his coat and gasped. The powder was not the only thing she'd left behind. One brow stuck to him like a caterpillar. She plucked it off, but he took it from her and looked quizzically at it. She snatched it from his fingers only to have him grab it back.

"Enough," he said after they'd transferred the thing back and forth a few times. "What the devil?" He stared at her face and without any warning ripped off the other brow.

"Ouch." She rubbed her stinging forehead. "My eyebrows are rather stingy looking, poorly shaped. I thought to enhance them."

He ran his thumb over the length of one of them. "They look exactly as they should to me. Suddenly, you have lashes, too. You no longer look like a white rabbit."

"Take off the cap," he commanded in a voice that no doubt had sent his military subordinates running to do his bidding.

When she didn't immediately comply, he yanked the cap from her head. Her golden-red hair slinked down past her waist like a silken shawl.

"Christ almighty."

He set her onto her unsteady feet. Tess sat down hard on the bottom step.

"Beadle, you must have something to do with this charade."

Beadle's ashen face crumpled. Before he could stammer an answer, Lord Marcliffe helped him roughly to the door. "Our business is at an end." He tossed the man unceremoniously into the night.

Lord Marcliffe turned and stalked toward her. "Who the hell are you?" He hadn't raised his voice, but the tone was chilling.

Tess glanced up at him, but his face was out of focus. She looked down at her ludicrous layers of clothing and sobbed. "Truth is, I have no idea who I am at this point. I would stay and figure it out for you, but I fear that if I do not return to my bedroom immediately, I will fall face first onto the hard floor."

She rose then zigzagged up the stairs toward her room. Blinded by tears, she yanked off her dress and flannel shift and sprawled atop the bed. Her life was unraveling disastrously.

Tess prayed Lord Marcliffe would allow her one more night under this roof.

℃

Tallon rubbed his thumb and forefinger together, still trying to rid himself of the feel of that bizarre furry thing she'd had plastered to her brow. She'd exposed perfectly shaped brows of a dark golden hue, brows he wanted to trace with his finger.

He did not bother announcing himself. The woman owed him an explanation, and, by God, he would have it. A pile of clothes stopped the progress of the door. He yanked at them, finding himself with a handful of her funereal garb and a nightgown. On the dresser, the wig lay like a dead thing. She was buried deep beneath the covers, oblivious to his presence. Her hair fanned out over the pillow, each lock a separate shimmering copper coil. He wondered if it felt as silken as it looked.

He sat with force on the end of the bed, pulling the bedclothes down, exposing the tops of her naked breasts. It failed to rouse her. Obviously, the amount of anguish she'd felt over the loss of her small fortune had been no match for the drink she'd imbibed. He brought the candle toward her face. Her eyelids twitched, but they did not lift. Her face was mottled and tear-stained. With a small mewl, she shifted in bed, exposing two perfect rose-colored nipples. Desire slammed through him, making his heart hammer in his chest. He wanted her now. This instant. He groaned as her nipples puckered in the cool evening air. With effort, he fought the need to clamp his mouth over those erect nipples and suck hard. His fingers itched to stroke her soft cunt and have her purr in his ear. He hungered to taste all of her, to have her spread her legs wide for him, to thrust his stiffened cock deep inside her.

"Wake up," he thundered, desperate at the need she inspired in him.

She jolted upward and almost instantly cradled her head like a hollowed eggshell. "Have you no mercy?" She moaned. "On second thought, the only merciful thing you could do for me right now is kill me, or at least remove my throbbing head."

72

"Do not tempt me, woman. It would be all too easy to snap your pretty little neck in two right now."

She seemed suddenly aware of her nakedness and tugged hard at the bedclothes, but he refused to budge.

She hugged a pillow to her breasts and scowled at him. Her narrowed eyes glittered like pale green gems in the candlelight. "Would you please put that out?"

"I should set the room ablaze with candles just to punish you for being such a deceitful wench."

"I am not deceitful."

"Right. Then I suppose the peculiar costume you've been wearing was merely the latest fashion?"

She swayed, nearly smacking her head against the headboard. "I was trying to fade away. I did not want people to take notice of me." Her voice was soft and sad. "Please leave me be."

"You'll be explaining this all to my aunt in the morning. I expect to see you downstairs at daybreak."

"You needn't worry, my lord. If you leave right now, I promise I shall be packed and out before the sun shows. I will not need to disturb your aunt at all."

"And no doubt you'll be flat on your back in Beadle's bed in a twinkling."

She hurled a pillow at him, which he managed to deflect. He leaned over her, his knuckles imbedding in the soft mattress on either side of her legs. He could smell the wine on her breath. He dipped his head and licked her lips. She gave a small cry of protest, which he ignored and swept his tongue over her mouth once again, revealing perfect, blush-colored lips. The powder tasted chalky on his tongue. She'd been masking her entire face in cosmetics. "You will be downstairs explaining your lies to my aunt tomorrow morning. Is that clear?"

A visible shudder ran through her body. Her powderless lashes, heart-stoppingly luxuriant and dark now, fluttered. "Fine. You are right, of course." Her lips pouted delectably. "I do owe her an explanation for my dishonesty."

"Glad you see it my way."

"But it wasn't all a ruse."

"Pray tell, Hortensia, which part was truth?"

"The part where I said I hated you."

"Now *that* I believe." He left the room, slamming the door so hard behind him, it nearly fell off its hinges.

Chapter Seven

Beadle had managed to rescue only two dresses from the collectors. The elegant wardrobe her father had had made for her first and only London season had been confiscated.

Because her spirits were low, Tess decided the blue dress would be the most appropriate. It was years old and barely reached her ankles. She'd grown in other places, too. She was unable to fasten the top two buttons. Her breasts were nearly spilling out of the bodice.

Dread crept up her spine. What would she do without money, or friends, or family for that matter? And debtor's prison seemed as much a threat as it always had. But she would not sink to putting on that cowardly disguise again. If the authorities wanted to pursue her, they could.

Mr. Rowland Beadle was as good as dead in her mind. She would probably have to take up employment in the bowels of some workhouse if she didn't want to starve. She chastised herself for not staying to explain her actions to Lady Stadwell, but her nerves were raw with fear and she felt a letter would have to suffice. Mostly, she could not bring herself to face Lord Marcliffe. He obviously despised her, and she could not blame him.

She stepped onto the stoop. The air was chill and smelled of rain. The weather matched the grimness of her mood. Tess pulled her cape tight around her shoulders.

She hadn't gone two steps on the drive when he rode up alongside her.

He glared down at her. In one quick motion, he dismounted and had her lone valise in his hands. The fine linen of his shirt clung to his sweating torso. A cheroot clamped in his teeth, he spoke out of the side of his mouth as he rifled through her bag. "So, Hortensia, what have you decided to *borrow* from my aunt's house?"

This was unbearable. Now he thought her a liar *and* a thief. "I would much prefer to starve to death than steal something from your aunt, or you, for that matter."

From her bag, he plucked out the only item she owned that held value to her. He weighed the smooth stone in the palm of his hand.

"Damn you. Put that back," she cried.

He exhaled. His eyes narrowed through the screen of smoke. He was inspecting her as he had last night, as if she were a stranger to him. Someone startling and new. "Amazing. You tell another truth." He dropped the stone back into her valise and thrust the bag at her without securing the clasp. "So you've taken nothing to see you through hard times, which leads me to believe you will be taking Beadle up on his offer."

"Perhaps, but he shan't be the last. There are far wealthier prospects in town."

His gaze raked over her. "Yes, I do believe you could make a fortune spreading those legs."

She slapped him hard across the face.

He stepped closer to her and pinched her chin between his

thumb and forefinger. He lifted her mouth to his and, for a spine-tingling moment, she thought he would kiss her. "I might even make you an offer myself."

His rude words snapped her abruptly out of her state of delirium. "You could not pay me enough to lie in your bed."

Abruptly, he dropped his hand from her face. "Have it your way. But before you hurry off to your glorious future, I will take you to speak with my aunt."

Refusing to meet his eyes, her gaze drifted away, alighting on the scarred ridge visible through the shirt made sheer with sweat. Her pulse raced. His battle marks reinforced his dangerous qualities.

He rubbed his shoulder. "You needn't frown so. I'm quite aware of how ugly the thing is."

"I am merely surprised that a man such as you brought so many souvenirs home from the war."

"A man such as me?"

"Black-hearted, ruthless. I thought people with that type of character could waltz through battles with nary a scratch."

"I much preferred your other incarnation. Not near so sharp of tongue. You'd best tame your mouth before you see my aunt."

"There is really no need for all that. I've left her a letter detailing all my defects."

Surprisingly, he took a step back as though in retreat. But then, he bent over and with one quick movement hauled her up over his shoulder. She felt like a sack of grain. Her hair nearly grazed the marble floor as they passed through the entrance hall.

The blood rushed to her head and she badly wanted to pummel the back of his thighs. "I thought I hated you before.

But now I truly loathe you. You are a churlish, insensitive beast."

"Coming from you, I consider that a compliment," he answered dryly.

He plunked her down outside the breakfast room doors. "You won't be going anywhere for awhile." With a rough pull, he tugged the ribbon of her cape loose and, before she could protest, he had the garment in his hands.

"Damn," he muttered. His gaze fixed on her breasts.

Tugging hard on the panels of her bodice, she attempted to fasten one of the top buttons. The action did not please him. Taking hold of her shoulders, he swiveled her around. With one big hand cupping her backside, he propelled her into the room. He followed so closely she expected to feel the scrape of his boot toe on the back of her heel.

Lady Stadwell looked up from her tea, her eyes widening. "Finally. She's perfect. You've done it. There will be no resisting this one."

Confused, Tess twisted her head around to look at Lord Marcliffe. His eyes were unreadable, his lips dipped sulkily.

"Perfect for what, Aunt?" he asked in an exasperated tone

"Sloan."

⯍

Tess's heart fluttered with hope and some trepidation. She slid into the chair next to Lady Stadwell. "Do you really think so?"

"Aunt, do you not recognize her at all? This is Hortensia. She's shed her cocoon."

Lady Stadwell lifted her quizzing glass and after a long moment said, "Hortensia, is that truly you?"

"I owe you an apology. I was not completely truthful with you. You see, Sloan has had a devastating effect on my life, as well. I am as eager to trap him as you are. Mr. Beadle convinced me that my coloring—"

Lady Stadwell picked up a strand of her hair. "Yes, your coloring is quite extraordinary."

"Mr. Beadle believed I would be too visible, too easy to find. He was to wrangle with my father's creditors while I took respectable employment. Now, I have nothing left to me but my need for revenge."

Lord Marcliffe cocked his brow in a most disconcerting manner. "Bravo," he said, punctuating his sarcastic remark with a languid clap of his hands. "A performance worthy of an award."

Tess mustered the fiercest look she could and directed it at him. And all she got for her effort was a broad-shouldered shrug.

Completely annoyed with him, she turned her attention back to Lady Stadwell. "My father got involved in Sloan's scheme. He invested far more than he could afford." Tess fiddled with the utensils atop the tea service tray.

Lady Stadwell stilled Tess's fidgeting by placing a hand over hers. "Poor dear."

Tess muffled a sob with her fist. She glanced up quickly to find that Lady Stadwell's eyes were also glossed with tears. Despite the skepticism radiating from Lord Marcliffe, Tess felt the sudden need to confide in Lady Stadwell. She removed the stone from her valise and placed it on the table. "I waded into the river three times to empty my father's pockets of rocks before I was able to drag him ashore." Tracing the black vein that ran through the pale gray stone, she allowed the tears to run unheeded down her cheeks. "My father mortgaged his farm to give me a future. He sacrificed everything for me." There was no need to disclose her real name. They did not need to know that her father was a viscount.

Lord Marcliffe thrust a handkerchief at her, and she shoved his offer away.

Lady Stadwell patted Tess's arm. The sympathetic gesture was belied by the enthusiastic sparkle in her eye. "Don't you see, Nephew? She is the answer to our prayers. This clever girl is what our plan has been lacking."

"She is too green. She will never hold Sloan's interest. He likes them well-rehearsed in the art of lovemaking."

"Perhaps my nephew is right. Would you be up to the task?" Lady Stadwell asked.

Tess's cheeks grew hot with shame. Would she really be willing to sacrifice her virtue to avenge her father's death? *Yes,* she thought with conviction. Her hatred for Sloan was without end, and now there was the additional incentive of proving something to Lord Marcliffe. "Absolutely," she replied.

"Then we will have her taught. Mrs. Midwinter will give her lessons," Lady Stadwell said matter-of-factly.

"No, I will not have it. Aunt, this girl has been lying to you since she arrived. How can we trust her now?"

Tess could feel the warmth of him as he stood behind her chair.

"Don't be ridiculous, Tallon. I trust her completely. She only did what she had to, to protect herself. You need to put aside your own desires and help us with this plan."

"My own desires? What are you going on about? This fixation with Sloan is not allowing you to think rationally."

Lady Stadwell waved away his objections. "It is quite settled."

༄

From the instant Tess joined Lydia Midwinter and Lady Stadwell in the parlor, she knew that going forward her life would be completely altered. If Miss Midwinter proved successful, the country-bred girl would disappear to be replaced by a temptress.

Lydia Midwinter, dressed in a dark gray silk that would have been prim had it not plunged dramatically, fiddled with an eyeglass strung on a chain around her neck. She daintily brushed cake crumbs from her fingers before raising the glass to her eye and scrutinizing Tess.

"Turn around." Lydia Midwinter sketched a circle in the air. Embarrassed, Tess pirouetted. "An innocent lamb," she stated flatly. The quizzing glass dropped, nestling again between her breasts. "As I feared I will have to start from the beginning. I've never corrupted a virgin before. I expect it shall be taxing, and I will require sustenance."

Without asking what she required, Lady Stadwell ordered wine and cigars be brought. For Lydia, it seemed, sustenance did not equate with food.

Tess wondered as she watched Lady Stadwell leave the parlor how two women from completely opposing worlds had formed an alliance. The question must have found expression on her countenance because Lydia answered.

"Lady Stadwell and I met at a most unfortunate event. A funeral. You see, we adored the same man. And much to our surprise, we found that we actually liked each other."

Lydia picked up a cigar and rolled it between her fingers. She swept it beneath her nostrils, inhaling deeply. "Where should we start?"

Though it seemed probable that Lydia was musing to herself, Tess offered an idea. "Perhaps with kissing?" She hoped to begin with something tame.

Lydia dismissed the suggestion with a wave of the cigar. "For some men—too many—kissing is merely a way to judge a woman's talent with her mouth. Lord Marcliffe happens to be such a man."

Tess was disheartened, but not surprised. No doubt Lord Marcliffe would be a demanding lover who would not care to spend time on anything so frivolous as kissing. What a waste of such inviting lips.

"Sometimes words can be misleading. I always think images help to clarify." From her reticule Lydia pulled an oversized fan, a bottle of an opaque black emulsion, foolscap and a small sponge. With a flick of her wrist the fan blossomed. The slats were made of ebony and clicked against the dark wood of the table as she set the fan down. Squinting through the eyeglass, Lydia Midwinter inspected the fan and with a nod, fed paper beneath it.

Curious, Tess leaned over and stared as well, but saw nothing except an intricate cutout pattern that reminded her of lace. The tip of Lydia's tongue showed between her lips as she concentrated on wetting the sponge with the paint-like substance and spreading a thin coat atop one of the slats.

With a triumphant smile, she pushed the stenciled image in front of Tess. It took a moment for the lines to form into an image Tess could recognize and when they did, she gasped. The fan was indeed unique. Carved with exquisite precision into the slats were acts of sinful escapades. The women presented were completely nude, but the men, naked and erect, wore tricornes or wigs. The device seemed to be a relic of a bawdier era.

"Don't worry, little lamb, I shall explain all. For now just enjoy the pictures."

Tess resisted the urge to pick up the paint-stained fan and flap air against her reddened cheeks.

Lydia took another carved slat and created a new lewd print. She pushed the foolscap across the table. In this tableau, the woman seemed to wince in pain, and Tess thought it no surprise considering the woman was being speared by massive erections. Depicted on her hands and knees, the woman's mouth was filled with one man's shaft while another man impaled her rear end.

Lydia ran her fingers around the lace of her décolletage and admired the print. "Quite the delicious challenge she faces."

Tess wondered if the expression on her face was as stunned as she felt. "Is this the usual way of it?"

"There are all sorts of ways. And some that still need to be invented." A wicked smile curled Lydia's lips.

Tess dared another question. "Is it true only men get pleasure from these acts?"

"While it is true that some men are rutting pigs, thinking only of their own desires, a good man makes sure everyone is satisfied."

After many hours of detailing the various sexual positions and how to respond to each and every touch and, more importantly, to each and every thrust, Lydia finally offered a reprieve. "Let us walk the grounds. I'd like to clear my lungs of London soot."

Hurriedly, before she could change her mind, Tess strode to the french doors and threw them open. The refreshing breeze helped to cool her overheated skin and sensibilities.

How freeing it was not to be encased in all that black. And how glorious it would be to tend the garden and feel the spring sun penetrating the thin muslin of her dress.

In the distance, Tess noticed the stable boy, Jem, chopping away at the hedges. A trail of massacred branches lay scattered a distance along the perimeter of the yard. Who had decided it wise to put a pair of clippers in the groomsman's hands? Likely the temporary master of the estate, Tess thought with annoyance. As they neared the boxwoods, Tess realized the rightness of Lord Marcliffe's decision. The groomsman was actually talented at sculpting the unruly plants.

Walking across the overgrown lawn dislodged a curl from Tess's chignon. She reached up to tuck it back into her bun and managed only to set more coils free. She'd worn the wig so long she'd forgotten how to dress her hair.

Lord Marcliffe sat on the bench, his Hessians propped on the gazebo railing. His muscular thighs bulged in the snug breeches. Her pulse quickened. What would it be like to have a man that size enact some of the scenes she'd studied? Which type of lover would he be? A selfish one, or one who gave pleasure? Tess could imagine him either way.

Lydia headed straight for the lounging lord. Apparently, it wasn't fresh air Lydia craved, it was an audience with the man who seemed to hold sway over every decision made in the house.

Lydia loudly praised the rather sorry-looking roses, and Lord Marcliffe turned at the sound, as he was meant to. He shot to his feet and snatched his coat from the back of the gazebo bench.

"Please do not don that stifling coat on our account, my lord," Lydia said.

He ignored her suggestion and jerked it on. The smile he offered was only for Lydia. He fished another cheroot from his pocket and offered it to her. Clearly, he was aware of her smoking habit.

Lydia gave a demure nod. He used the glowing tip of his cheroot to light hers. They both puffed on their cheroots. Their expressions remained passive, and their voices were barely audible, yet they seemed to be arguing.

Feeling as though she were eavesdropping, Tess took a couple steps away into the shadow of the ash tree. She could sense Lord Marcliffe's anger by his stiff posture.

With his handsome profile to her he managed, somehow, to have eyes in the side of his head. "Very wise not to mar that ivory perfection, Miss Calloway. Leave that to Sloan."

"I am not standing here to avoid freckles. I simply prefer not to be intimidated. I see how you've bullied poor Jem. He should be the one tending the horses. But instead he's gouging holes in the garden. You must control every situation." Tess was not about to encourage Lord Marcliffe's arrogance and admit that Jem was doing a good job.

Lydia gave Tess a quelling look. "Do not bait him so, my dear. You serve at his pleasure."

"Exactly," he agreed.

After his smug response, Tess half expected to see his mischievous dimple make an appearance, but his expression remained sulky. She decided to ignore him and began working the pins from her hair. The weight of the lopsided bun was starting to make her scalp ache.

"I see your aunt's assessment was correct. Lord Marcliffe, you seem quite opposed to the plan," Lydia said.

Lord Marcliffe glanced pointedly at Tess and she shifted deeper into the shadow of the tree. "It's not the plan so much as the lure."

"But the lure is so very alluring." Lydia laughed at her wordplay. "As I see you've noticed. Such stunning hair color," she offered. "Dainty waist." She drew a curve in the air. "Ample breasts."

Lord Marcliffe shrugged. "They could be larger."

"I've never known a man to prefer them smaller," Lydia said with a smirk.

Tess had to bite her tongue. She wanted to scream at both of them for treating her like an object that needed to be perfected so it could perform properly. But she couldn't completely dismiss his assessment. Were her breasts truly too small?

She swept her curls from her shoulders and almost sighed at the sensual feel of her hair gliding over her skin, a sensation her disguise had denied her. Discreetly, she squeezed her arms against her sides, plumping her breasts and creating a deeper cleavage. She supposed she must take Lord Marcliffe's word for it because she had no notion what a man considered ideal. She glanced up from her inspection to find him staring at her, or more specifically, at her breasts. And he was certainly not viewing them with disinterest. His dark blue eyes glinted with a wolfish gleam. When he lifted his gaze, she frowned at him.

Unrepentant, he continued to study her openly. "Besides she's a virgin." The last was a question masquerading as a statement. His chest heaved with a visible intake of breath, which he did not immediately expel as though he were waiting for Lydia to confirm the state of her chastity. Why, she wondered, did he feel he had a personal stake in her virginity?

She could hold her peace no longer. "How is that any of your bloody concern?"

"I'm certain she is a virgin." Lydia addressed Lord Marcliffe as though Tess hadn't spoken. "But these arts can be taught, which is exactly why your dear aunt has called me here."

His shoulders relaxed. "Miss Calloway is not thinking with her head, just her heart."

"You should have more faith, my lord. I assure you that many secrets have been spilled in bedchambers. And to that end, I would like to contribute something to the seductive trap being devised. A bed of the most ingenious design, inset with scrolled ironwork that most would assume was merely ornamental. With a bit of silken rope a woman can present herself in the most startling ways." Lydia sighed dreamily. "Imagine binding wrists and ankles to the headboard."

"A man like Sloan doesn't stop with a bit of rope," Lord Marcliffe responded. "Look at her hiding under the tree. Do you think her a match for a man like that?"

Tess stepped forward. "Tell me the worst about Sloan so I'll know what I'm facing."

Lydia gave her a sympathetic smile. "You will find Sloan as smooth as cream, but he can sour upon further acquaintance. It is best not to cross him. I recall the widow Treadingham refusing him. Treadingham served in your brigade, did he not, Lord Marcliffe?"

Lord Marcliffe did not respond, but Tess could not help noticing that his lips were set in a grim line.

"Sloan found a way to pollute her wine with crushed rhinoceros horn or something equally vile. But to be serious, the powders he uses are of a black nature. One in particular made from a beetle certainly brought the widow to her knees, so to speak." Lydia cupped her gloved hand over her lips, but a hoarse laugh escaped her. "When the women left the men alone to their cigars and port, the widow did not budge. And once surrounded by masculinity, she proceeded to lift her gown and petticoats above her hips and brace herself against the table, offering herself to all the men present."

"Poor thing." Tess pressed her chill fingertips against her fevered cheeks.

Lydia said, "Do not feel too much pity for the widow, dear. Sloan does not always distinguish between friend and foe. He has been known to ply his mistresses with those very same elixirs until they are as compliant as slaves."

Tess's knees buckled and she sat hard on the gazebo bench.

"Do you recall that wicked dinner party, Lord Marcliffe?"

Lydia's hint was far from subtle. Tess wished she could cover her ears with her hands and blot out her words. She did not wish to hear that Lord Marcliffe had taken part in the debauchery. He did not utter a word in his defense. He tossed his cheroot to the ground and snuffed it out with the heel of his boot.

"Do not blush so on Lord Marcliffe's behalf, dear. The earl was not present at the table that night. The gossip reached my ears, but was quickly doused. There were tales of an angel, a fellow army comrade who came to the aid of the poor widow's reputation." Lydia hinted unnecessarily with a sly wink.

And doesn't he look every bit the hero, Tess thought as an opportune breeze stirred his shiny black hair. She preferred to forget that only moments ago she'd imagined him taking part in the widow's downfall.

"There were threats of duels if the outlandish tale were ever whispered of again," Lydia continued.

"And yet you speak of it," he said with arctic calm.

For once Lydia looked cowed. "Only this once. To let the girl know with whom she is dealing."

Chapter Eight

In a week's span, the single walk to the garden was the only time Tess had enjoyed daylight under Lydia Midwinter's tutelage. The parlor, their own little schoolroom of iniquity, was now littered with sticky wine goblets and cigar stubs. Strewn across the table were the erotic prints.

When class was finally dismissed, Tess waited for Lydia to exit the room before gathering the prints and tossing them into the fire. The very thought of Lord Marcliffe coming upon those explicit pictures made her stomach flutter. The first stop Tess made was the kitchen, where she set the large kettle to boil. She would steep herself in hot water and scrub away the smoke.

Later, delighting in the fresh, soapy scent of her hair, Tess felt presentable enough to join the others for afternoon tea. After greeting Lady Stadwell and Lydia, Tess strode over to the sideboard, poured some tea, snatched a couple of cucumber sandwiches and settled herself at the table. She was certain a permanent blush stained her cheeks. Her mind was still spinning from all she'd been taught. She'd had no idea such things existed between a man and a woman.

When Lord Marcliffe walked in she tried to look everywhere but his face and instead found her gaze drifting far lower, taking the measure of him. Would she really be expected to use her mouth to pleasure a man—there? Her tongue flicked the corner of her lip. He seemed to grow before her eyes, hard and rigid. She quickly lifted her gaze to find him staring at her with a narrowed, accusatory glare.

He yanked out a chair and sat down. He glowered at her from across the table. "Aunt, don't think for one moment that once Sloan has bedded her that he will impart any information. The only dialogue he'll have with her is to ask her price."

Tess lifted her teacup and found that her hand was trembling. The tea sloshed onto the snow-white linen. With a clatter, she replaced it on the saucer. "The earl thinks that all men's minds work as his does."

Judging by the sneer on his lips he did not find her the least bit witty. "You have no idea what you are entering into here, sweeting. You may think me a bastard, but I assure you that once you are in Sloan's grasp, you will think only hell could be worse."

Miss Midwinter took a ladylike sip of her tea. "'Tis true that Sloan is more than a bit perverted in his proclivities."

A shudder ran through Tess. It did not go unnoticed by him. Very little she said or did went without his notice of late.

She found herself watching him as well, taking surreptitious peeks over her teacup. He was clad in the same coat and trousers he'd worn at dinner the night before. They were badly creased, and she wondered if he'd slept in them.

"You smell as if you've bathed in whiskey," Lady Stadwell said, seemingly oblivious to the crude conversation they'd been having.

In response to his aunt's admonishing tone, he tipped back his chair so it balanced on the back legs and snatched the decanter of liquor from the sideboard. Landing his chair on all fours, he drained the contents of his teacup into the floral centerpiece then proceeded to fill the cup to the brim.

Tess could not recall seeing him sober since the cheerless conversation in the gazebo.

Amazingly, the whiskey appeared to do nothing to diminish his appetite. He ate heaping forkfuls of egg and steak, the strong muscles of his jaw working as he continued his unrelenting scrutiny of her. But Tess found that every bite she took lodged in her throat. She felt as though she were on personal display for his amusement.

Into the tense atmosphere, Mrs. Smith ushered a guest.

"Captain Gibbs, my lady," Mrs. Smith said.

The man swept off his hat, making his brown hair stand up in tufts. He had an engaging smile. "Lady Stadwell, a pleasure." As his gaze circled the table, his gray eyes widened at the sight of Lydia Midwinter. Then he was staring at Tess, his handsome smile broadening.

Lord Marcliffe got to his feet to greet him. "What brings you here, Gibbs?"

"An invitation from your aunt. Damn, Cliffe, you look like—"

"Death," Lord Marcliffe completed the sentence. "Feel it, too." He poured himself some more whiskey and dropped back into his chair.

"Getting an early start, eh?" Captain Gibbs said.

"Never stopped." Lord Marcliffe took a healthy swallow from the cup.

"Did you read my note?" Lady Stadwell asked as Mrs. Smith served the captain tea.

The captain took the vacant seat beside Tess and looked pointedly at her. "Yes, and I wish to volunteer my services for this endeavor."

Lord Marcliffe started drumming the table with his fingers. "What's this about?"

"Insurance, nephew, insurance. We are investing too much in this plan to have something go wrong. We've established that Sloan wants what others have. And you and Captain Gibbs have always been objects of his envy, which explains why he was so intent on winning over your mistress, Miss Sparkes. Heaven knows there is little else about the woman that could have interested him."

Tess had to smile. A blunt tongue was what she loved most about Lady Stadwell.

"Your disdain for Miss Sparkes has never been a secret." Lord Marcliffe's impatience was clearly growing. His fingers picked up a faster rhythm. "Could you please focus on why Gibbs is here?"

"You must have lost a great deal of blood on that battlefield, my dear. You've been quite muddled of late. It is all very obvious. For the plan to work, Miss Calloway must be kept by someone Sloan considers a rival. Since you have shown so little enthusiasm for this project, Miss Midwinter and I thought to enlist Captain Gibbs."

Tess gasped and brought the napkin to her mouth, but not before momentarily drawing everyone's attention to her. Lord Marcliffe's attention lingered longest. Tess wished the table was smaller or her leg was longer so she could give him a hard kick. Damn him for completely dismissing the plan. Now Lady Stadwell had brought a stranger into the deal. If Lord Marcliffe had no role in tricking Sloan then he'd have no reason to stay.

"Besides, Miss Sparkes would not be pleased," Lydia said.

Tess had heard more than enough about the earl's mistress. Miss Sparkes had boasted of his talents to Lydia Midwinter and Lydia, in turn, had obviously felt it her duty to pass along those intimate details to Tess.

Captain Gibbs moved closer so that the sleeve of his coat brushed Tess's arm as he reached for the sugar bowl. "Miss Calloway, have we met before? London, perhaps? The Hampton's party more specifically? There was a beauty in London a season ago who had just such rare coloring. An exotically plumed bird who made the other females look like drab sparrows by comparison."

"Alas, I've never been to London." The man had such an open and earnest face that it actually pained Tess to lie to him.

"Exotically plumed birds find themselves easy prey. They get eaten." Lord Marcliffe, who was ever alert to any contradictions in her story, had managed to pick up on the least important part of the captain's conversation. A steady diet of whiskey, Tess surmised, did not improve a man's skills of perception.

"Have you been drinking as well, Captain? Birds and plumes, whatever are you two talking about?" Lady Stadwell asked.

"Gibbs, you don't want to get involved in this."

"But I assure you, I do." Captain Gibbs bestowed another beaming smile on Tess.

Lord Marcliffe swept his cup and saucer aside and leaned menacingly across the table. "I assure you. You do not."

Captain Gibbs still had a charming, innocent smile plastered on his face as he pulled his gaze away from Tess and glanced at his friend across the table. When he saw the look Lord Marcliffe was giving him, the smile melted into a grimace and the color in his cheeks drained.

Lord Marcliffe got up from his chair abruptly. He grabbed the edge of the table to steady himself. "I will be the man to whom she belongs."

Relief washed over Tess.

Captain Gibbs held up his hands in a gesture of surrender. "I was only trying to help, Marcliffe."

"If you want to help, you can start by talking these women out of this mad idea," Lord Marcliffe said as he lurched out of the room.

∞

The modiste arrived not long after Lydia Midwinter and Captain Gibbs had departed. Tess and Lady Stadwell spent the rest of the day ensconced in the parlor deciding on patterns and fabrics for a spring wardrobe.

The next morning, Tess woke to find herself tangled in her blankets. She'd been dreaming of satin and silk and erotic couplings. The explicit pictures that Miss Midwinter had shown her were branded on her brain. A woman bound with ropes, lifting her bottom in offering as she waited for the man to plunge into her. A woman servicing three men at once. Miss Midwinter had added her own narrative, describing the sexual acts depicted so graphically Tess had been forced to open the window to the chill morning air to cool her cheeks. All her lessons lacked were practice. Her dreams had revealed a deep hunger for that real experience. Unfortunately, in every dream Lord Marcliffe was the man she explored with her mouth and hands and body. She'd slid satin over the smooth skin of his chest until it snagged on the rough scars of his shoulder. More shockingly, she'd followed the trail of the fabric with her open mouth, her tongue tracing every ridge.

Frustrated, she threw her bedclothes aside. She stepped naked out of bed and bathed herself at the washstand. After patting herself dry, she opened the wardrobe and peered into a dark and empty hole. Not even her chemise hung there. She searched the floor, shook out the bedclothes, got on her knees to peer under the bed and found nothing, not a stitch. Even the flannel gown she'd thrown off in the night was gone. She wrapped herself in a blanket. Opening the door a crack, she called for help. No one answered. Her pleas seemed to echo off the walls.

Tess stepped into the hallway and raced down the stairs. There was a queer emptiness to the house. She shivered as her bare feet touched the cold tile floor of the entrance hall. With the heavy blanket dragging behind her, she entered the dining room. No weak tea or burnt toast awaited her. She pushed open the kitchen door expecting to see Mrs. Smith's smiling face, only to find another vacant room. Afraid now, she hurried up the stairs to Lady Stadwell's bedchamber. The door was ajar. She found the wardrobe empty as well as the bureau drawers.

She'd been deserted. She could not go into the yard naked, but she was certain what she would find there. No gardeners, no grooms, and the stable cleared of all horses.

Without question, she knew exactly who had executed this plan, who'd evacuated the house right under her nose. Trembling with fury, she returned to her chamber. Why not take advantage and luxuriate in bed for once? First she fluffed the pillow but then decided to give it a good pounding, until feathers burst from its seams. She settled back on the now flattened pillow, but finding rest in her agitated state proved impossible. With a scream of vexation, she kicked the covers to the floor then with a muttered oath stooped to retrieve the blanket. She had yet to explore Mrs. Smith's room. Determined to thwart the fiendish earl, Tess lit a candle and ascended the servants' stairs. The flame fluttered eerily in the narrow hallway. Muttering a plea for fortune to turn in her favor, she entered the low-ceilinged room. The doors on the small wardrobe were agape, and the barren interior that greeted her seemed a purposeful taunt. Not even a blasted apron remained.

Sparked by another idea, she raced downstairs to see if the mudroom that adjoined the kitchen held at least a rain cloak. The hooks were empty. The bastard had been ruthlessly thorough. If he wanted rid of her so badly, why hadn't he left her some clothing? Clearly, he wished to see her completely humiliated.

She stomped through the empty house. In the parlor, she clutched at the faded damask drapery thinking to yank the curtains from the wall, but the curtain rod was too heavy and well-seated. She would have to take scissors to the fabric. It was an inspiration with little chance of success. Her skills as a seamstress were negligible. Besides, it would take her forever to create a garment. She glanced out the window at the stables. Though the house was somewhat isolated, certain angles of the yard could be spied from the road, and Tess did not have the courage to go outside mantled only in a blanket. When night fell, she'd fetch the ladder from the barn. She would explore the attic for moth-eaten garments. Surely there had to be remnants of other generations stored. Unable to occupy her mind with reading or anything remotely productive, she curled up on the settee to wait for dusk.

Chapter Nine

The sky was just starting to gray, the gloomy veil of night dropping, when the front door slammed. Tess flew off the settee and raced into the entrance hall, her bare feet skidding on the slick marble, to find the devil himself, with the two huge mastiffs at his heels. He gave her a placid smile as he pulled off his leather gloves. What was he up to? She didn't trust a hair on his black head.

"W-What is going on? Where is everyone?" she stammered, completely flustered by the idea of being alone with him.

"They left early, just before the sun. I had the cook accompany Lady Stadwell in the carriage so that people would think you'd left with her."

She eyed him suspiciously. "Why would you do that?" Her voice rose to a hysterical pitch and he immediately pressed his fingers to his temples.

Though he appeared stone cold sober, he was suffering the aftereffects of a week of imbibing. His skin was paler than usual and in stark contrast to his black hair. "Because people talk. And since we are just beginning this venture, I felt there was no need to stir up rumors."

Tess pulled the wool blanket tighter, scratching her bare skin. She had never felt so vulnerable. She blinked up in confusion at the most intimidating man she'd ever known. She was at his mercy. Lady Stadwell had abandoned her.

"Is there some reason—" With effort, she squelched the urge to rain curses down on him "—why I have nothing to wear?" Her voice vibrated with fury.

He shrugged. "The dressmaker will have some of your wardrobe completed by the week's end. In the meantime, you won't need any clothing."

"I suppose I'm to lock myself in my room naked until she arrives?"

"No, I expect you to stay in *my* room naked for the week."

She couldn't have understood him correctly. "Pardon?"

"If I'm to hire you for my aunt's dubious scheme, I'd like to see just how capable you are."

"Exactly what does that mean?"

"I intend to fuck you, Miss Calloway."

Lord Marcliffe was studying her a little too carefully. She suspected he was expecting she'd lose her nerve. He casually combed back his windblown hair with his fingers. How on earth could someone be that handsome and that cruel? "I detest you!"

"Yes, you've made that clear."

"I thought I was to be transformed into a mistress, not a whore."

"To my mind, there is only the finest line between the two."

"Don't you think you are taking this a little too far? I only needed someone to pretend to be my lover."

"So you were just going to pretend with Sloan, as well?" With his tinderbox, he began lighting the candles studding the enormous candelabrum on the entrance hall table.

Tess chose to ignore his barb. She was determined not to

think of Sloan until the dreaded moment came. She started up the stairs. "Go away. I will manage this myself."

"Ah, then you are prepared to pay the modiste and the rent on the London townhouse?"

She paused. Her pulse beat in her throat and in the palm of her hand where it clutched the railing. She glanced over her shoulder at him. He already had the candelabrum in hand, clearly intent on illuminating their way to his chambers. His jaw was set in a stubborn, firm line.

His question, of course, was rhetorical. She had no options but to obey him. Why waste breath on futile arguments? The whole plan would collapse without his aid. "Fine then, we'll do it your way."

She heard him snap his fingers to keep the dogs from following. Her back stiffened as she sensed him behind her. "I know you think to dissuade me with this threat, but it will not work."

On unsteady legs she made her way down the hall to his chambers. All she could think after he'd closed them both in the room was that the man had a heart of black ice. He set the candelabrum atop the night table, but the glowing lights did not add cheer.

She turned to him with a defiant smile.

His head tilted slightly to the side, an odd, rather boyish expression on his face.

Clearly, he hadn't expected her to submit. Wouldn't he be shocked, she thought, to know that she would have eagerly acceded to his demands if he hadn't approached it in such a high-handed manner?

The glint of surprise winked out of his dark blue eyes almost immediately. "Confident little baggage, aren't you?" he said.

"I intend to succeed at this, no matter what it entails." Her body, though, seemed to have different ideas. For all her bravado, she found herself back at the door, her hand on the latch. "First, may I get you something to eat?" she asked, hoping that acting the good hostess could forestall things.

"That won't be necessary."

"Whiskey?" A hint of desperation broke through the light tone she attempted.

"I don't want food, or drink, or a smoke. Just get in bed."

Was she going to be the only one naked in this enterprise? He hadn't even taken the knot out of his cravat. Perhaps this truly was a test with no real interest or passion on his part. "Is this how you do it then? Only the woman undresses?"

"Not normally." The muscle in his jaw twitched. "But I know my scars disturb you." He lifted his gaze from her body and stared into her eyes. He seemed to accuse her of callousness.

"What gave you the notion that they disturbed me? It is only that I had never seen the like. They are fascinating and frightening all at the same time."

Lord Marcliffe studied her from beneath heavy lids. He did not take her words as an invitation to remove a single article of clothing. She had to commend herself on being quite the seductress.

Apparently, he was expecting *her* to initiate the session. Tess moved toward him.

"Somehow, this wool blanket does not add to the passion of the moment." With a flick of his wrist, he removed the blanket and threw it halfway across the room.

His hungry gaze slid over her. "I'll be damned. It seems every layer I peel off reveals something astonishing."

Her nipples puckered in response. Wedging her bare feet between his Hessians, she rubbed up against the fine fabric of his coat. The man was so compelling that she could almost forgive his arrogant behavior. Had her heart ever beaten so fast? Lord Marcliffe, even fully clothed, was the most tempting man she could imagine. But it wouldn't serve to let on that she found him irresistible. She had to match his callous indifference with her own.

He dipped his head suddenly, and she turned her face away before he could press his lips to hers. Hadn't Miss Midwinter mentioned that he preferred the sex act without kissing? Besides, she didn't want to open her heart to him and somehow kissing seemed more intimate than anything else they might engage in tonight.

"Shall we proceed?" she said.

He traced her collarbone with his finger. "How would you like it, sweeting?"

Her eyes fluttered shut with the pleasure of his touch.

"Against the wall perhaps? Like a waterfront doxy." His harsh words were like a splash of cold water. Obviously he was determined to make this as difficult as possible.

"Perfect," she shot back. Tess gave him an insolent look. If he thought he was going to intimidate her out of this, he was wrong. Unfortunately, she could not stop from trembling beneath his intense gaze. For a fleeting moment, she believed she saw tenderness in his eyes. *Only wishful thinking*, she chided herself. His gaze dropped from her face and raked the length of her naked form. There was no mistaking this look. It was decidedly carnal, completely possessive and wholly without mercy.

His hands spread over her bottom and pulled her against his muscular body. Something dauntingly big and hard pressed against her stomach. He lowered his mouth to hers.

She turned her face again. "No need," she said. "I'm aware you don't care for kissing."

He seemed amused. "Is that so?"

"Your mistress complained to her friend, Lydia Midwinter. Besides, Lydia said that unless I wanted to lose my heart to some cold-blooded man—" With the last words she gave him a pointed look. "—it's best, when given the option, to not practice it much." Quite possibly, she'd drive him off soon with all this blather. "Not that there is a chance that I could ever fall in love with you," she added to make certain everything was perfectly clear.

She could see in the set of his jaw that the last of her feather-brained speech had angered him.

He lifted her up, walked her over to the bed and plopped her unceremoniously in the center of it.

She lay back and propped her head on the pillow. Her nakedness made her extremely self-conscious. She kept her legs pressed together, her arms at her sides, fists clenched.

His mouth quirked into a nasty smile. "Midwinter is quite the tutor. Sloan would be laughing hysterically and kicking you out on the street by now."

From the night table, he removed a flask of liquor and made a wordless offer of it. Like a woman dying in the desert, she seized it. She took three greedy swallows of the stinging liquid.

He plucked the flask from her. Raising his brows, he gave it a shake as if measuring the contents. "Damn, I merely intended to loosen you up, not knock you senseless." He capped the bottle and tossed it aside.

Grabbing one of her ankles, he pulled her toward the end of

the bed. Her legs now dangled over the edge. She propped herself on her elbows. He placed her feet on the edge of the bed and then spread her knees apart. All the erotic pictures in the world could not have prepared her for this experience. With shock, she realized she could see herself in the full-length mirror across the way. She thought she could see everything until with his thumb and forefinger he spread her nether lips wide, exposing the pink folds of her sex. He turned his head and his eyes met hers in the mirror. The look he gave her was so intense she was sure she would swoon.

This was all happening too fast. She tried to push her knees together. With a rather rough grip on her leg, he hooked one ankle on the outside of the bedpost. She was completely open and exposed to him. The night air whispered over her flesh but could not cool the heat pulsing between her legs. The alcohol was already working, helping to lessen her inhibitions.

Lord Marcliffe's thick black lashes fluttered downward. His eyes were now focused with a heart-pounding intensity on the pink, swollen lips that lay beneath the golden curls. His breath sounded ragged.

"You have a beautiful cunt."

This wasn't all business to him after all.

She stayed propped on her elbows watching in the mirror as he stroked the pink, increasingly moist folds of her quim. He pinched the small, protruding nub and an exquisite sensation thrummed through her. With the callused pad of his thumb, he stroked her there, over and over again until she was shaking. Tess was frustrated that he was still fully clothed. She wished she could touch the naked muscles of his shoulder and to see his black hair graze the bare skin of his neck.

Her arms gave out, and she collapsed back onto the soft mattress. He loomed over her. She watched with shock as he brought his fingers dipped with the cream he'd inspired to his lips. He smiled a devil's smile. And then he dropped to his knees between her trembling thighs. His teeth clamped gently down on her nub, and he nibbled. Tess thought she would die from the fierce pleasure.

Modesty propelled her to bring her legs together again. His black hair felt like silk against her skin. He brought her hands down and placed them on her inner thighs.

"Keep your legs splayed for me," he commanded.

Tess obeyed him as spasm after spasm made her clench her quim against the delicious onslaught of his tongue delving into her inner folds and then licking up inside her. He dipped his finger again into the cream, which dripped down to the crack between her buttocks. Then he inserted the tip of his finger into her tight, puckered hole while his rigid tongue thrust into her quim. He pushed his finger in deeper and deeper still, until it was completely inside her.

At the invasion, Tess's body shivered with ecstasy. All her senses were concentrated on his long finger impaling her anus and his tongue dipping into her. He pulled his finger out and then thrust it in again, pushing it farther still. A foreign, exquisitely sweet feeling shuddered through her body. Releasing his hold on her, he finally allowed her to bring her knees together. She turned to her side, curling in on herself, the delicious sensation still pulsing through her body. Obviously, he was one of the good men whom Lydia Midwinter had mentioned. She glanced up at him and noticed that his gaze had not softened and amended her thought immediately. He had clearly not satisfied himself.

Weakly, she crawled beneath the quilts. He finally threw off his coat and waistcoat and untied his cravat. In invitation, she peeled back the cover beside her. She wanted to be held. All of sudden, she was desperate to be close to him. After he had thoroughly explored every inch of her, the only touch that seemed important to her now was to be wrapped within his arms. Instead, he sprawled into the chair near the bed, his mood dark and forbidding. Her heart ached.

"As enticing as you are, you are a novice in the art of seduction. A man like Sloan would see through the ruse immediately."

It was a devastating comment. Clearly, nothing about the experience had pleased him. "But that is unfair. You gave me no chance to seduce you. Perhaps I need someone to teach me how to handle a man."

"You are looking at the someone."

"I meant someone kinder."

"Go to sleep," he said, his voice raw with some indefinable emotion.

The harsh regard of those dark blue eyes was the last thing Tess remembered before falling asleep.

Chapter Ten

Tess stretched, the fine linen sliding over her naked body. The sheets on his side of the bed remained untouched. Sadly, she had been the only occupant of the bed last night. Thrown over the back of the chair where he'd taken up his vigil was his greatcoat. She remembered with a blush that besides his gloves and cravat, the coat was the only thing he'd removed. She stuck her arm out from beneath the warmth of the coverlet and dragged the heavy wool garment atop the bed. Burying her face in the coat, she breathed in his scent. She'd done it now. All her resolve to seduce Sloan and bring him to justice seemed insignificant in comparison to her feelings for Lord Marcliffe.

Still under the covers, she slipped her arms into the sleeves before braving the chill air in the chamber. The coat weighed down her shoulders as she wrapped it around her and fastened the cravat at her waist. The sound of a whip cracking startled her and she moved to the window to pull back the heavy damask curtains.

Lord Marcliffe exercised his massive horse on a long tether. Tess flinched as he cracked the whip against the dirt and the stallion arched its back and leaped into the air.

The whip slapped the ground again. The menacing sound made her feel jittery. His control over the horse brought to mind his mastery of her body. She yearned to experience him again. Restless and hungry, Tess decided to make breakfast.

Once in the kitchen, she folded deeper cuffs in the sleeves to keep them from the flame and put the kettle on to boil. She rolled out a batch of scones and whipped some honey into clotted cream. Her mind was so preoccupied with the godlike earl who'd knelt between her legs that she ended up baking enough for a small regiment.

The door opened and she heard his boots on the stairs. He sounded as if he were taking them two at a time. Suddenly, the hunger was gone and her stomach was twisting into knots. Her hands trembled as she placed several scones and a bowl of clotted cream onto a tray. Swallowing hard, she tried to work up the courage to face him. She felt feverish just thinking about his tongue caressing her so intimately. He bellowed her name, and she nearly dropped the tray. She realized she'd never heard him raise his voice before. Counting to ten, Tess hoped to slow her pulse. It was important to appear confident or he would never believe she was up to the task of seducing Sloan.

Lord Marcliffe was at the top landing, gripping the railings, scrutinizing her every step up the staircase. He pointed behind him to the open door. "Naked and in my bed. Is that really so difficult to remember?"

"So I'm to languish in your bed with no nourishment?"

"Naked and in my bed," he repeated, as though she hadn't spoken.

"Do you know, you sound very much like a barbarian shouting those simplistic phrases?"

She pushed past him into the bedroom and shoved the papers on the desk aside before setting down the tray. The slam of the door jolted through her.

Feeling a little barbaric herself, she didn't bother with a

knife and plunged her scone into the clotted cream. "I'm not taking off this coat until you put some coal on the grate."

She did not turn around to see how her demand was received, but the sound of coal hitting iron echoed through the room.

Tess felt heat penetrating the thick wool coat though the fire hadn't taken hold yet. He reached around and slid his hand into one of the pockets. Her breath quickened as he withdrew a slim, velvet box. A card which had also been in the pocket fluttered to the floor. Tess glanced at it as she picked it up. It was a note from Captain Gibbs written on the back of a calling card.

He placed the velvet box on the desk. "Open it."

A string of diamonds sparkled up at her. It was the loveliest necklace she'd ever seen.

"Beautiful. But why?"

He shrugged. "Jewelry makes the mistress."

Tess fastened the diamonds around her neck. The stones felt cool against her skin. "I see. These will give me some legitimacy with Sloan." She instantly knew that her comment had angered him.

"Take off the coat." His tone had returned to the cold one he'd used the night before.

She saw no point in disobeying him. Her trembling fingers fumbled with the tie at her waist. "You can stop growling at me. I will not be intimidated."

She slipped the coat from her shoulders, folded it carefully and placed it atop the divan. Shyly, she lifted her eyes. The look he gave her was so intense, so possessive that she found it hard to breathe. The diamonds draped around her neck made her feel decadent, and her naked skin tingled.

She plucked the calling card from the desk. "I see from Captain Gibbs's note that you may expect him today. Have you changed your mind? Will he be given the dubious honor of being my protector?"

"Would you rather fuck Gibbs?"

She could feel the color drain from her face. "That would be fine."

He cocked a brow in question. "Is that why you look ready to cry?"

Damn her trembling chin, always a dead giveaway that tears were on their way. "For your information, I am not about to cry. And any woman would be honored to be escorted by someone as *kind* as Captain Gibbs."

"*Escorted.* Is that a euphemism Mrs. Midwinter taught you?" He twitched the card from her grasp and tossed it away. "So you don't think I am kind? I gave you an expensive necklace."

"If you are so impressed by it, then why don't you wear it?"

He reached for her and her nipples puckered in anticipation, but he only picked up one of the gems and rubbed it between his thumb and forefinger. "You seem to be getting more pleasure out of these jewels than you profess." The surly half smile on his lips made it clear he was aware her body's response was due not to the necklace, but to him.

Determined to shock him out of his cockiness, she dipped her finger into the honeyed cream and settled herself on the divan. Tess pillowed her head on the folded black coat then swirled the cream around her erect nipple.

His fierce gaze nearly made her lose her nerve.

"Lydia says that men enjoy dessert." Proud of her audacious behavior, she coated her other nipple.

With three fingers he scooped a generous dollop of the cream. "I know Lydia did not neglect to mention that the cream should go here as well." He transferred it to her fingers and nudged her knees apart. She let them fall wantonly open. Gently, he manipulated her hand, causing her to stroke the cream into her slit. A scintillating sensation crawled up her naked back.

An adorable yet cunning smile tipped his lips. She looked up at the wildly handsome man ready to devour her. Miss Midwinter was certainly learned on the subject of men, she thought.

"Really," she said, "we should just put an end to this particular lesson. It would be easy enough to fake pleasure. Obviously, we've proven Lydia's little trick has merit." She closed her knees.

He nudged them apart again. "You must stop making a habit of that." He leaned over and blew gently across her nipple, and instinctively she arched her back toward his mouth.

"I see you have become quite skilled at faking pleasure," he drawled.

He lowered his head and took the entire areola in his mouth and sucked hungrily. She purred with pleasure as she dug her fingers into his silken black hair, desperate to draw him closer. He moved his mouth to the other breast. When he lifted his head, both nipples were glistening, pink and erect.

"My lord." Her voice sounded breathy and far away. "No need to go further—" she said, just as one of his long fingers drew through the cream slathering her slit. He brought the cream to his mouth.

"You know how tempted I am by sweet things." His heavy-lidded eyes were glazed with desire. He dropped to the floor at the foot of the divan and caressed the cream into the pink folds of her sex. Her surroundings blurred as she concentrated only on the exquisitely intimate touch. His head dipped and with an open mouth, he made love to her quim.

She'd never felt anything so wicked in her life as his tongue stroking her hungrily. Moaning softly, she lifted her eager bottom to meet his thrusting tongue. After a sinful series of kisses so deep her body pulsated with pleasure, Tess clutched at the divan and cried out. When she opened her eyes, he was standing over her, staring at her with something akin to fascination.

"You are surprisingly responsive," he said. "You do hate me. Right?"

"Very much," she said cheekily and got to her knees. She reached for the fastenings of his pantaloons.

He caught her hands, stilling them. "What are you doing?"

"I would think that was obvious."

"Why are you doing it?"

"A virgin courtesan would not have any credibility." She punctuated the statement with an unconvincing laugh. She peered up into his beautiful blue eyes and the truth came spilling out. "That's merely an excuse. I've wanted to touch you since I first laid eyes on you. I dream about touching you...tasting you."

Those were the magic words it seemed because without delay he undid the breeches himself. Daringly, she shoved them off his hips and slid her hand down into his drawers. Her hand wrapped around his thick, hot cock. He threw back his head with a primal groan. His cock throbbed in her hand. She smoothed her hand over the sleek skin to the base, to the crisp black hair and then back again to squeeze the fleshy head in her fist.

"Careful, sweeting, this might lead somewhere you're not

111

ready for."

His warning only made her bolder. She tugged the ribbon loose on his drawers and pushed them off as well. She moaned at the sight of his erect cock. It had been imposing in its flaccid state, but now it was dauntingly big. He was so hard everywhere, so completely masculine. She curled both hands around him and pumped.

"Like this," he instructed and guided her hands with his own, correcting the rhythm and pressure of her strokes. His head was bowed, his black hair falling forward. They both watched as her hands slid over him.

She moved one of her hands to his balls and squeezed as she continued pumping his shaft. "Am I doing this correctly?"

His chest was heaving. "Enough lessons for one day."

"You're the teacher." Reluctantly, she dropped her possessive hold on him, but not before swirling her thumb around the cream on the head of his cock. She brought her thumb to her mouth and painted her bottom lip as though applying rouge.

He groaned, seeming to anticipate her next move. She wanted to taste him, and with enjoyment licked the cream from her lip.

With a rapidness that stole her breath, he scooped her off the divan. She clung to his neck as he swung her around and pressed her against the wall. Instinctively, she straddled his waist.

She rubbed her cheek against the rough stubble of his jaw as she whispered in his ear, "Against the wall just like a waterfront doxy."

They both stiffened at the sound of the dogs barking and Gibbs trying to shout over the noise of the excited animals.

112

A sigh shuddered through his entire body. "Damn that bastard. He never knocks."

With a groan, he set her on her feet. He yanked up his pantaloons, scowling as he adjusted his still-erect cock.

He stalked across the room to the washstand, filled the basin from the pitcher and nearly submerged his head in the water. From his wardrobe, he chose a cutaway coat then looked down at the bulge in his breeches. "No, that isn't going to work." He shirked off the cutaway and reached for a frock coat. He buttoned it and combed his fingers through his wet hair.

"Did Lydia coach you to say that to me? To tell me you wanted me?" He regarded her through narrowed eyes.

Still hurt that he hadn't held her the night before, she decided to leave him guessing and offered only a sly smile in response.

&

"I *knew* she looked familiar." Gibbs slammed his fist on the end table. "I have a talent for faces. Especially extraordinary ones."

"Hortensia?" Dunking his head in the chill water hadn't helped to cool the fever she'd inspired.

"Her name's not Hortensia. It is Tess. Tess Starling."

"What the hell are you talking about?" His patience was quickly running short with Gibbs.

"Stop your bloody pacing, and I'll tell you." With a smug look on his face, Gibbs sat back, spread his arms across the back of the settee and waited.

Suspicion growing, Tallon stopped mid-stride. "Speak."

"Do you remember how last spring Lord Kempstone was in a complete lather after spying a particular viscount's daughter at the Hampton's ball?"

Everyone that season had been aware of Kempstone's obsession with the beauty being offered on the marriage mart. And Kempstone had been far from the only admirer of Tess Starling. Tallon shrugged, although he felt anything but unconcerned. "I never met her."

"Ah, yes. Spent most your time in the clubs avoiding a couple of matchmakers who were willing to risk their precious offspring with you." Gibbs turned his head and stared at the parlor's entrance. "Where are all the bloody servants? I'm parched."

Tallon walked across the room to where his aunt kept her cognac. He strode back and thrust the glass and decanter at Gibbs. "It's not the same girl," he insisted.

"I'd bet my left ballock on it," Gibbs said.

"You had better keep them both. God knows you are pitiful enough with the full package."

Gibbs, who had been sipping his cognac, sputtered into his glass. "Very amusing."

"Do you think you might get back to the subject of Tess Starling?" His uneasiness grew. He'd never known Gibbs to tell him anything other than the truth. This would explain why Tallon's solicitor had had no success with his inquiries regarding Mr. Calloway and the settling of his debts.

"Yes, quite right," Gibbs replied. "Lucky girl, slipping away from Kempstone. Can you imagine having to listen to him blathering on about his hunting triumphs?"

"Your point, Gibbs?"

Gibbs, not feeling the least bit rushed, poured himself

another cognac and swirled the amber liquid in his tumbler. "Well, Tess Starling's father had underestimated the cost of a season. She'd barely been in town when he whisked her back home. Poor devil died not long after. There were whispers of suicide. I believe the girl was the one to find him." He took a small item from his waistcoat pocket. "I knew you'd want proof." He set the item carefully on the table between them as though it were a precious egg. "It's Kempstone's lucky talisman. Had it on the table at the gaming hell."

Tallon lit a candle before lifting the oval porcelain box from the table.

"Careful, Kempstone will have my head if anything happens to it."

Tallon held it up to the candlelight. The artist had captured her exactly, including the beginnings of that seductive smile of hers. He doubted there was a man who saw that painting who didn't wish he'd put that satisfied smile on her face.

"A portrait her father had commissioned, but then he didn't have the blunt to pay the artist. Kempstone had it made into a snuffbox. The fuss he made over my borrowing it, you'd think I'd asked him to lend me his wife." Gibbs sat forward and peered at the box resting on Tallon's palm, admiring it anew. "Damn delectable handful, that one."

Tallon gave his friend a quelling look. His fingers folded around the snuffbox. He wanted to crush it. She'd tricked him again. He was keeping a viscount's daughter as a veritable slave to his desires with all intentions of making her his mistress. "I'll get this back to you," he said as he stood.

Gibbs eyed Tallon warily. "Remember, it will be my head or worse," he said.

"At least you will still have both ballocks. See yourself out, will you?"

Gibbs chugged back his cognac. "That's gratitude." He plucked his top hat from the arm of the settee and set it firmly on his head. "Remember, don't dare lose that box," he warned again before leaving.

Tallon raced up the stairs. Her need for revenge and his own selfishness had done him in. But he was not so far gone, become so amoral, that he could not see his place in this, could not find his way out of this pit he'd dug for himself.

Stubborn as always, he thought, she'd appropriated his coat again. Curled atop the divan, she'd fallen asleep over the book she'd been reading. Luxurious lashes shaded her creamy pink cheeks. She was irresistible.

He leaned over her. "Hortensia." She didn't rouse. "Tess," he amended.

Her thick lashes fluttered open, and she reached up and stroked his face. She was getting accustomed to him. The thought made his heart jump. Wild tendrils of her copper-colored hair framed her face. She smiled at him, a wicked variation on the shy, seductive smile captured in the miniature portrait.

"So, *Tess Starling*, would you like to tell me why you lied to me, again?"

The smile vanished as she sat bolt upright, knocking her head against his chin.

She rubbed her head. "Who told you my name was Tess?" She pouted her bottom lip and he had the urge to bite it.

"Turns out Beadle was right. Your coloring does attract unwanted attention." He could not resist picking up a long strand of her hair and wrapping it around his finger. "You'd become quite the favorite while you were in London."

She scooted away from him. "I do not understand how my true identity is any of your business. It really doesn't change a thing."

"Hell yes, it does. It changes every damned thing. I will be arranging a wedding in the morning. I have enough black marks against my name, I do not need to add another." He rubbed a hand over his face. "Seducing a viscount's daughter, that's a new low for me."

"You have clearly lost all reason, Lord Marcliffe. I have no intention of marrying you."

He shrugged, but he did not feel indifference to her words. The muscles in his jaw jumped. "Your intentions be damned. You will become my wife."

"I want Sloan—I mean I want to hurt him—to destroy him. He ruined my father, as he did your uncle."

"I am sure your father would not have you sacrifice your own future."

"Don't you see? I am the reason my father lost everything. He wanted to give me a chance. He wanted to find me someone suitable to marry."

Her amazing green eyes regarded him cautiously. She looked beautiful and vulnerable, and he had to suppress the urge to scoop her into his arms. "By suitable, you mean wealthy?"

"You cannot fault him. He wanted an easier life for me."

"Well, his wish will be fulfilled when you marry me."

"You must forgive me, my lord, for being a little dubious about your suddenly *honorable* attitude. After all, you've kept me naked and vulnerable for the past few days. I would ask you not to decide my life for me."

His gaze moved meaningfully to the bed. "And the time we spent together?"

Suddenly, she was looking at him with huge, glossy eyes.

"This week has been a complete lie. You were never intending to go along with your aunt's plans."

"Did you really think I would procure you for that bastard?"

"What of the women you interviewed?"

"I was putting on a show for my aunt. I figured she would come to her senses once she had women who made their living fucking traipsing through her house. Unfortunately, she is as stubborn as you are."

She winced at the vulgarity of his language. "But you arranged for a house in town. You paid for a wardrobe—" she touched her fingers to her neck "—and jewels."

"I wanted you." The words came out before he could stop himself. "Only now I'm prepared to make you my wife instead of my mistress."

"I'm not yours for the asking, Lord Marcliffe."

"But you *are* Sloan's for the asking." He reached out and pinched her chin between his fingers. He lifted her face so she was forced to look him in the eye. "You are quite the little bitch. You should do well in your new profession."

She slapped his hand away.

He could feel himself clenching his jaw with anger and a more foreign feeling of jealousy. "My aunt will be returning on Friday. I will let her decide what to do. I am through with you and your deceptions."

She tore off the necklace and hurled it at his retreating back.

He turned hard on his heels. "Keep it. Think of it as payment for allowing me between your legs."

Chapter Eleven

After her refusal of his proposal, Tess took to her room. On Friday, after days of sneaking around the house trying to avoid Lord Marcliffe, she woke to find her wardrobe doors ajar. The closet held three beautiful new garments. Voices below brought Tess to the window. Lady Stadwell had returned.

Tess walked over to the washstand and tipped water from the ewer into the basin. The cold water and the fresh scent of the soap helped to wake her. Without the aid of a mirror, she ran a brush through her dampened curls and fashioned her hair into a chignon. From the closet, she snatched a morning dress. Wearing it was a necessary evil. She had two choices: either remain naked or wear a dress he'd purchased for her. On her way to the door, she stepped over the discarded necklace. The diamonds seemed to wink up at her. Tess swiveled on her heels, plucked the glittering strand from the floor then headed downstairs to wait for Lady Stadwell's verdict.

߯

As expected, her audience was not with Lady Stadwell alone. Lord Marcliffe clearly thought his aunt needed protection from her devious lady's companion. He lounged in a chair, his hand wrapped around a glass of whiskey which was propped atop his thigh. She walked over to him and dropped the sparkling gems into his liquor.

"Thank you, but I prefer my drinks without ice," he said as he set his glass aside.

With some urgency, Lady Stadwell motioned her over. "Is it true, my dear? You are the daughter of Lord Starling?"

"Yes, but—"

"I thought you said your father was a farmer."

"Most of his tenants had moved on. He tried to tend the land himself, but he was not terribly successful."

Tess found it hard to ignore Lord Marcliffe's presence. He'd gotten up and now loomed over his aunt's chair, a dark, forbidding figure. As black as his reputation was, he had not shied away from what he felt was his duty. An earl, no less, and far richer than her father's wildest expectations. But she didn't want to be anyone's duty. Particularly not his.

"Does the girl remain untested, Nephew?"

"She does." The look he gave her was accusatory, as though she'd denied him.

Satisfied by her nephew's answer, Lady Stadwell relaxed back in her chair. "I understand your father wished to see you settled properly."

"What father wouldn't want that for his daughter?" Tess replied.

Lady Stadwell lifted her hand in a silencing motion. "Then that is what we will accomplish." It came as a shock to find that Lady Stadwell was willing to put her need for revenge aside and refused to sacrifice a girl raised in a genteel household to her plan.

"I've had a week to think things through. With a little help from my *conscience*." Lady Stadwell gave her nephew a teasing look. "The scheme was fanciful. It would never have worked. And we certainly aren't going to use a well-born young lady as a lure."

"So the only reason now that you are against the plan is because I'm a viscount's daughter." Society's ridiculous rules, Tess thought. Only minutes before he knew her true identity she would have been perfectly suited as a mistress to Lord Marcliffe and now because of her parentage she was marriageable material.

"It is an arrogant way of looking at the world, but old traditions are hard to break," Lady Stadwell said.

Tess had just been exposed to a world of eroticism that she'd had no notion even existed. And she had never felt less a viscount's daughter. She'd left herself unguarded both physically and emotionally to prepare herself for what was ahead. And she'd done it all for nothing.

Lady Stadwell pursed her lips and Tess wanted to laugh. Here she'd been the architect of this unseemly plan and now she was playing the proper matron.

"I feel as if I've been betrayed and used badly here," Tess said and looked pointedly at Lord Marcliffe.

"I've made it clear that I never approved of this plan," he said.

Certainly, his rough behavior at the beginning of the week had been meant to scare her off. "I know I was stubborn, and you tried to dissuade me...in your own unique way. Yet, you are not completely blameless."

Lady Stadwell shot him a knowing look. "My nephew is rarely completely blameless. But all of this has no bearing anymore. I'm taking it upon myself to find you a suitable match. Allow me to right the wrong I've done," Lady Stadwell said. "Besides the modiste is working on the rest of your new wardrobe. It would be a shame to waste it in the country. Though I don't know what you will do with those rather revealing nightrails Lydia designed for you."

"Wear them for my new husband," Tess suggested with a shrug. Tess felt a relief that she shouldn't have. She blamed herself for that weakening of resolve.

"Or you could donate them to the nearest brothel," Lord Marcliffe said with a chillingly clipped tone.

Tess dared a glance at him. He looked hard and distant. Fascinated, she watched as his long, beautiful fingers plucked a thin, dark cheroot from the cigar box on the table. Biting her lip to suppress a moan, she thought about those fingers pushing deep inside her. He brought the cheroot to his lips, and her gaze followed. She wondered what it would be like to kiss those lips. She would never find out now. Last night, fired with the sudden, startling realization that she'd fallen in love with him, she'd lashed out. And after her spiteful refusal, she had sealed her fate. He would not be renewing his proposal. Now she would be put on the marriage mart. Lady Stadwell's charm and persistence would almost assure Tess a mate. And she would spend the rest of her life wanting Lord Marcliffe.

છ

"I've no doubt this dinner party will bear fruit, Tess, dear. I know of at least three very suitable single men who will be in attendance."

Tess hid a smile as she adjusted the seams on her gloves. Lady Stadwell had suggested the very same rosy scenario on three different occasions that week alone. So far all the single men had been more suited in age for Lady Stadwell.

The courtyard was alight with torches. The parade of

guests stepped cautiously over the slick cobblestones still wet from the afternoon rain shower. Tess sighed heavily, dreading the night which was sure to be a repeat of the past soirees. Another night of dreary conversation. Another night of dull card games and overcooked food. Another night without Lord Marcliffe. Tess glanced back at his glistening black carriage and her shoulders drooped. She missed him dreadfully.

They'd barely stepped foot in the ballroom when Lady Stadwell was whisked away by one of her matronly acquaintances and Tess, finding herself alone, scouted out a dim corner and tucked herself there. Maybe if she were lucky no one would even notice her and she might be able to skip dinner altogether.

"Miss Starling, is that you?" The question boomed over the laughter and enthusiastic chattering of the small crowd.

Tess winced at being singled out in such a manner. With little regard for those in his path, the man barreled toward her. The candlelight reflected off his spectacle lenses making it difficult to see his eyes, but she recognized the pointed nose and pronounced chin. The eyeglasses were the only thing bookish about the man. Her brief London Season was coming back to her now. Lord Kempstone on her heels like a hound dog and cornering her at every function. She hoped he'd spare her the details of his latest hunting expedition.

Lord Kempstone sniffed and pushed up his spectacles with his forefinger. "Yours is the last face I'd expected to see here. It was as if you'd vanished. I'd contacted your father's man of business, a Mr. Beadle, concerning your whereabouts and he had no information to give me."

"I left London rather unexpectedly," she said.

His thin, pitying smile told her that he was well aware of her father's demise. "I, myself, have only just returned from a romp in the lake country. An abundance of water fowl in those parts. Ducks, geese. The sky is nearly dark with them. A hunter's paradise. And as you know, I consider myself quite the bird man. A mere three days in the field and I had bagged two dozen of the fattest."

Tess nodded weakly. She tried her best to show her interest, but her gaze kept wandering across the room to a stylishly dressed man with thick blond hair and a disarming smile. His presence seemed to have caused somewhat of a stir, and he conversed with everyone with charming familiarity. Over the heads of two giggling women, he caught Tess looking at him. He started to cross the room toward her. She shyly dropped her gaze.

"Kempstone, I understand your wife's looking for you in the next room." And then the blond man turned his dazzling grin on Tess, who showed her gratitude with a return smile.

Lord Kempstone cleared his throat and nodded politely at Tess before going off.

So Lord Kempstone had found a woman to appreciate his monotonous narratives, Tess thought. She was relieved he was no longer in search of a mate.

"You looked like you needed rescuing." The man's tousled, pomaded curls reminded her of a finely carved bust, and his side-whiskers were precisely trimmed. Her heart ached for Lord Marcliffe's midday stubble and shaggy hair.

With the bold stranger standing only inches from her, Tess's niche no longer felt so safe. "Yes, thank you, I'm very grateful." Before he could introduce himself, she sidled past and went in search of Lady Stadwell.

"There you are, child. Pray, don't leave my side again tonight." Lady Stadwell flicked her fan wildly. "Such a dreadful evening we have before us. You will never guess who has been invited to dine." Her gaze darted around the room. Leaning toward Tess, she used her fan to shield their conversation. "The villain himself. Sloan."

Lady Stadwell fluttered the fan again, and Tess seized her wrist to stop the movement. "I've never met him. Which one is he?" She glanced from one small group to the next.

"You're not still thinking, dear, that you will somehow get involved with him? Lord Marcliffe will never forgive me if I allow such a thing."

"Lord Marcliffe is not my keeper." At that moment she realized her hatred for Sloan was still keen. She'd come this far, why not continue with the plan and avenge her father's nightmarish death?

"If it were not for my nephew's generosity I'm afraid your circumstances would be very different."

"I do appreciate all he's done," Tess said as she scrutinized the men in the room. The man who had come to her rescue earlier still seemed to be eyeing her from across the room, and the smile that had at first struck her as charming seemed altogether insincere now. Of course, the man had to be Sloan.

Lady Stadwell seemed to realize that Tess had already picked him out of the crowd. She grabbed Tess's gloved hand. "My nephew was correct. My plan was ridiculous. I was not considering the danger you would be in. Please, Tess, let's not give it another thought."

"The heartache he's caused both of us is worth the risk." Tess gave Lady Stadwell's hand an affectionate squeeze. "You needn't worry, I will give him no occasion to injure me further. And I will see that he does not leave any other ruined lives in his wake." Tess shot a look in Sloan's direction. He appeared to be deep in conversation with an elderly couple. His expression constantly shifted, alternating from raised eyebrows to quirked lips to a toothy grin. He appeared to be fascinated by every word the couple uttered. "I assure you the beast is at this very moment searching out his next victim."

Lady Stadwell's pale eyes looked near to tears. "This is all my fault. If I had not put the notion in your head—"

"Pray, do not torture yourself, Lady Stadwell. You have been nothing but kind and generous toward me. The choices I make are my own."

"My nerves. I am sure I will not be able to swallow one bite at the table this evening." Lady Stadwell pressed her hand against her waist.

"You will make yourself ill. I won't do anything foolish. You have my promise," Tess assured her. But truthfully, she was not feeling completely sure of her own actions. When it came time to seduce Sloan, she was not completely convinced she would have the stomach for it. The only man who had ever touched her intimately was Lord Marcliffe, and she could not imagine anyone except him ever touching her.

As soon as Lady Stadwell's attention was diverted by an acquaintance, Tess disobeyed her wishes and left her side. Tess wandered to the pianoforte and plucked a booklet of music from the stand. She peered at him over the top of the pages. And when he sensed her notice, she dropped her lashes in a slow, flirtatious fashion. She managed to catch his eye twice more before dinner was announced. Tess was certain her tutor, Lydia Midwinter, would be proud.

The expected invitation was made. "May I be so bold as to escort you to the table, Miss Starling?" The silky voice came from behind. Sloan crooked his arm in offer. She could feel the warmth of his skin through the sleeve of his coat. It made him frighteningly real. She forced a smile as they followed the others into the dining room. This was it. The opportunity could not have presented itself more easily, and yet she wanted to dash from the house and run into the wet night. With a gallant flourish, Sloan pulled out her chair. Ignoring the grumbling of the man for whom the hostess intended the seat, Sloan plunked down beside her. Tess didn't dare look in Lady Stadwell's direction because she knew her vexation would be great.

Hoping for courage, she took a long sip of wine and then another. "How is it that you know my name? I am at a disadvantage, sir, for I do not know yours."

"I fancy myself quite the researcher. If I find something that interests me, I am quick to learn all that I can about it," he said.

"So this evening I have become the subject of your research?"

His smile was greasier than the dressed pigeons on the platters. "In a sense. I am William Sloan. I once did business with a Viscount Starling. Are you related?"

Hearing her father's name from his lips made her want to slap him. She set down the goblet in fear she would snap the delicate stem. "He was my father." Her words were barely audible.

"Yes, sorry to hear about him. I'd heard he'd suffered a reversal in fortune."

Tess wanted to scream. The gall of the man talking about her father as if he had not been the reason for his suicide. His callousness only served to reinforce her resolve.

"I understand you are a house guest of the Earl of Marcliffe." The man was a wizard at prying. No doubt he'd gleaned all the important bits of gossip with one stroll around the ballroom. "Did he appoint himself your guardian?" A sinister twist of his lips defined what was meant by the word "guardian".

Her cheeks reddened at his insulting suggestion, particularly because there was truth to it. She had so very nearly become the earl's mistress.

His eyes widened in mock innocence. "I meant no disrespect, I assure you," he lied smoothly. "I only thought, because of your orphaned state, that Marcliffe had taken you under his wing."

"I have not seen the earl since I arrived in town. I am visiting with his aunt, Lady Stadwell." Tess swirled her fork through her food, too queasy to actually taste any of it. "Are you an acquaintance of the earl?"

"We attended the same university, but I soon learned that it was best to avoid his company. And I advise you to do the same. He has the honor of a highwayman."

"If I happened upon a highwayman who resembled Lord Marcliffe, I'd welcome being robbed," the woman next to Tess said with a laugh.

The man across the table shook his head. "Frightful wound he suffered in Spain."

Soon, the number of enemy soldiers Lord Marcliffe had dispatched was bandied around the table.

"'Tis a pity how some of these lords rewrite history to suit their own glory." Sloan followed his bitter words with a grin.

Lord Kempstone peered around his wife and frowned at Sloan. "Bad form, speaking of a man who ain't here to defend himself." Lord Kempstone's timid-looking wife gave him a discreet nudge with her elbow, and he sat back in his chair.

Tess lowered her voice so that only Sloan could hear her and batted her lashes for effect. "Do you suppose all the valiant tales I've heard of Lord Marcliffe were the inventions of the man himself?" If she could betray the man she loved, then she might be ruthless enough to succeed.

128

"Sad but true, I fear. If you knew the man better, an intuitive girl such as yourself would quickly see through his lies."

Tess brought a gloved hand to her throat. "Your compliment is most undeserved. While I do consider myself clever in some small way, I assure you, I am not keen enough to see through layers of deceit if they are presented as the truth." With luck, by the end of the dinner, Sloan would be convinced that his newest conquest was the naïve daughter of a viscount. He raised his glass in silent toast to an elderly woman who was bedecked in sapphires and diamonds. Never had she met such a loathsome man.

The entire ride home, Lady Stadwell lectured her about the dangers of the scoundrel she was cozying up to, while Tess was preoccupied with the means she'd used to gain points with Sloan, siding with him against Lord Marcliffe, practically agreeing that the man could not live up to the legend.

Chapter Twelve

Frustration from the long, tedious ride had set Tallon's teeth on edge. It was a trip he could have made in half the time if not for his horse's temperament. The clamor of London made Dante unmanageable. The instant the rented cab pulled up before the townhouse Tallon leapt to the street. He did not bother announcing himself at the door. Instead he walked around to the garden, unlatched the gate and entered through the french doors. He found Cyrus slumped in a parlor chair, snuffling in his sleep. The room was chill, the hearth grate empty. Tallon nudged Cyrus with his boot, and the big man shot to his feet.

"Wasn't expecting to see you in town so soon, Major, sir. I mean, your lordship."

Tallon smiled. After serving for so long as his sergeant, Cyrus found it hard to shake old habits of address. "My aunt, is she away?"

Cyrus smiled, his eyes crinkled in mirth. "Aye. And the lass ain't here either. Went to the Gray's for yet another ball."

Tallon headed to his chambers and yanked fresh linen and a tailcoat and trousers from his wardrobe and tossed them on the bed. After washing away the dust and sweat of the day's travel, he soaped his face and with unsteady hands he wielded a razor.

Pressing his fingers to the nick on his throat, he called down from the landing, "Cyrus, do me the favor. I'm cutting myself bloody."

Cyrus thumped up the stairs. He took the razor with a chuckle and followed Tallon into the room. "You look as if you've murdered yourself."

Cyrus slung a towel over his shoulder and wiped the blade clean on it. Eyes narrowed in concentration, he scraped the razor along Tallon's jaw. "Never seen you this way, sir. You are in a lather over this one."

"I have unfinished business with the chit." To say the least. Unfinished business before the altar and unfinished business in the bedchamber, and not necessarily in that order.

Cyrus wet the towel and dabbed the blood from Tallon's face and stepped back to admire his handiwork.

"Excellent." Tallon stroked his freshly shaven face. He peered into the small mirror on the wall above the washstand and smoothed back his hair with dampened fingers. His hands still shaking, he turned up his collar and took the cravat from the bed.

"Would you go with wrinkled linen?" Cyrus plucked the cravat from his fingers. "Jane will see to your neck cloth. If you don't mind me saying so, sir, you could use a valet."

"Are you volunteering for the job?"

"Perhaps."

Tallon slipped on his waistcoat. "I don't recall a Jane."

"Your aunt hired her just this week. Chatters on a bit too much, enough to give me a blasted headache. But she's an industrious sort." Cyrus snatched up the top hat on his way out the door. "This could use a good brushing.

"Have the stable boy fetch the trap," Tallon called after him.

The cold night air in the open vehicle lashed back his hair but did not cool the fervor in his veins. He tugged on his high collar, pulling it away from the sensitive skin of his throat. Barely keeping his mind on the road, he sped toward his destination. His rapid maneuvers through the chaotic streets brought him the ire of fellow drivers. But he was too busy rehearsing his speech to pay but passing notice.

The line of carriages extended the length of the street. Tallon dropped down from the trap and took his hat from the seat. He adjusted his neck cloth and strode with purpose toward the front door. Though uninvited, he was ushered in by the servant with an obsequious bow.

Tallon stood at the edge of the room and scanned the crowd, nodding absently at those who greeted him. It took him only a moment to spot her. Beadle was right about one thing. Her coloring was brilliant.

His aunt was suddenly beside him. She seized his arm and steered him toward the refreshment table. Laden with unappetizing fare and bowls of insipid punch, it was completely abandoned.

"She has demurred all overtures...except one," Lady Stadwell said.

The words made his heart thunder in his chest. "Kempstone?" Tallon still possessed the porcelain snuffbox. He had no intention of returning it. If he wouldn't accept payment for it, then Kempstone would get it back in shards.

His aunt's mouth pulled into a sour frown. "Not Kempstone. He's found himself a partner. Though he has a tendency of forgetting his mouse of a wife whenever Tess is present." She signaled theatrically with her eyes that someone was approaching Tallon from behind.

A heavy hand clamped onto his shoulder. Tallon turned

and found himself face to face with the golden boy. Sloan was attired like a gentleman, but there was something too slick, too oily about the presentation. His teeth gleamed in a boyish grin. "Marcliffe, I thought you hated these things."

"Some nights more than others," Tallon said dryly, though he thought a fist through the sparkling smile a more appropriate response. But he would not humiliate his aunt. She wanted Sloan's misdeeds to be punished, yet she did not want a connection made between her and the man. Only a very tight circle of acquaintances knew that he had taken her husband for a small fortune.

"I heard you tired of that pretty little mistress of yours. Miss Sparkes, was it?"

What Tallon wouldn't give to remove Sloan's smirk permanently. "I suppose the fact that she is available makes her less interesting to you."

Sloan's nostrils flared. "Truthfully, I prefer something shiny and new." The last was said in a hushed voice with an eye to Lady Stadwell. He moved to the table and filled two cups with punch. "If you will excuse me, Lady Stadwell," he said with a dip of his head and hurried away.

The ominous tone of his aunt's words finally registered. *Except one.* And then he watched as Sloan presented a cup to Tess. Her pale green eyes glittered up at him as though she were gazing at the stars.

Tallon's hands curled into rigid fists.

"'Tis an act, nothing more. She means to catch him at something. She will not be dissuaded." His aunt placed a comforting hand on his arm. "Pardon my indelicacy. Almost from the moment we arrived in London, he was intrigued. Once he had an inkling that you might be her benefactor, he was drawn to Tess like a magnet. Just as I had predicted."

At that precise moment, Sloan looked over at him. With a self-satisfied grin, he raised a silent toast with the cup of punch. Tallon had never broken a man's neck with his bare hands, but he thought now would be the perfect time to try his talent for it.

"I think it best you go home, Nephew."

He removed his aunt's restraining hand from his arm. "Not just yet."

"Miss Starling," Tallon said as he approached.

She swiveled around and punch splashed out of her cup just missing his feet. She blushed to the tips of her perfect little ears, looking soft and kittenish and wholly adorable. She flicked her fan open and began fluttering it in front of her pink cheeks. "Your aunt has missed you." Her voice was barely above a whisper and her eyes seemed to plead with him not to give her away.

"It is nice to be missed," Tallon responded.

He could feel Sloan's agitation at the few words they exchanged.

Sloan shifted closer to Tess so that his arm grazed hers. "Your career as a soldier is still the talk of the town. We thought, Miss Starling and I, that perhaps your exploits were a bit overstated. I certainly cannot fault you, for what man would not make himself bigger than life to attract female admiration?"

"I would imagine there must be numerous topics more interesting for you and Miss Starling to discuss." Tallon attempted to catch her eye, but she refused to look at him, confirming that she had indeed spoken against him. Her betrayal sliced through him.

"I do hope I will not have to face down that rather grim attitude when I come to call on Miss Starling."

Undoubtedly, the bastard was anxious about Tallon sharing a townhouse with Tess. Tallon hesitated long enough to see both worry and a freakish excitement play across Sloan's smug features. "I'll be staying at my club in town," Tallon finally responded.

"The music is starting again." Sloan crooked his arm and she set her gloved fingers atop his sleeve. She did not even spare Tallon a backward glance as Sloan escorted her to the dance floor.

∞

Tess stepped expectantly into the house. The first thing out of her mouth would be an apology. It made her ill to think of her encounter with Lord Marcliffe at the Gray's party. The expression on his face had been plain to read. He'd been shaken by her betrayal. Tess would make him the vow she had made herself. Never again would she sacrifice him for the sake of cozening up to Sloan. To besmirch his reputation as a soldier was beyond ugly. The man had risked his life in service to his country.

Cyrus met them in the entrance hall. Lady Stadwell had a spring in her step that had been absent almost the whole of the evening. "Please inform my nephew that we are home."

"His lordship has come and gone, my lady. He is staying at his club."

Tess was thankful Cyrus had spared them the truth. Why would a man go to a stuffy men's club when he had a mistress who longed to lavish attention on him? Tess's deceptive behavior could only increase the appeal of Miss Sparkes.

The hopeful gleam dimmed in Lady Stadwell's eyes. "Perhaps it is better that he is not here. For we are off on

135

another adventure of which he would not approve."

"It is only a little repast in the Vauxhall Gardens. Certainly nothing one could approve or disapprove of," Tess said.

"You will not be wandering down any of those lovers' passages, my dear, of that you can be sure."

Tess found her first and only amusement of the night. Not but a few weeks ago, Lady Stadwell had inducted a courtesan to teach her the sinful arts, and now her virtue was sacrosanct.

Wishing only for the night to end, Tess trudged up the stairs to splash water on her face. Far more energetic footsteps soon followed behind. Tess knew it was Jane. The new maid seemed to be around every corner.

With a sigh, Tess turned to the maid as they reached her bedchamber door. She was in no mood to be fussed over. "Jane, please fetch Lady Stadwell her blue cashmere cape." Jane hesitated for a moment, her thin lips tightening perceptibly before doing as bid.

At the washstand, Tess filled the basin from the ewer and roused herself with the cool water. She lifted her head to find, dangling from the mirror's scrolled corner, the very same necklace she'd hurled at Lord Marcliffe. A soft moan of yearning escaped her as she recalled how he'd looked at the party in his elegant evening dress. He had been every inch the earl tonight. Utterly polished, with each gleaming black hair in place. Equally swoon-worthy as the rough warrior and the highborn gentleman.

Tess reached up and fingered the brilliant stones. Was this meant as an overture? Or a taunt? What if he had come to London to renew his proposal? No, she was just torturing herself with fanciful notions.

From her chignon, Tess pulled curlicues of hair to frame her forehead. She stared at her reflection. This new role she was playing, even without the disguise, felt less real than Hortensia. To have this revenge was costing her everything else she wanted. She'd even traded on her love for Lord Marcliffe to sidle into Sloan's life.

Appalled with herself, she turned away from the mirror and grabbed her warmest coat from the wardrobe.

By the coach, acting as footman, was the gallant giant. Cyrus politely helped her into the carriage. There was something comforting about his presence. Lady Stadwell, already seated, was fixing the blanket across her lap. The wheels creaked as the big man climbed up to the box. Curious, Tess thought, that Cyrus would be attending them this evening. Obviously, Lord Marcliffe had enlisted him to keep Lady Stadwell safe.

Sloan awaited them outside the gates of Vauxhall Gardens. He lifted a quizzical brow at the sight of Cyrus. "They're making lady's maids larger than they used to."

"Cyrus served with Lord Marcliffe in the army," Tess said.

"How interesting," he responded.

Hundreds of twinkling lamps gave the pleasure gardens a mystical quality. Cyrus guided Lady Stadwell along the illuminated paths. Playing the innocent flirt, Tess accepted Sloan's arm with a shy smile.

He patted her gloved hand. "I believe you were being coy when we first met. It is apparent that Marcliffe does not think of you merely as his aunt's houseguest. The way he stared at you, he hardly concealed his desires. When it comes to you, my dear, I'd say fire runs in his veins." Sloan leaned in close. Tess could feel his breath fluttering her hair.

She congratulated herself for not pulling away. "I believe you are just toying with me, sir. I hardly know the man."

"I must say he looked as sleek as a blooded stallion this

137

evening. And I did not notice any perceptible limp, though I have heard he exhibits one on occasion," he continued.

The man's assessment of the earl stunned Tess. He'd viewed Lord Marcliffe in much the same way Tess had. Did a man speak of another in such a fashion?

Sloan gestured toward a vacant supper box. "Ah, here we are."

Even considering her dinner partner, Tess looked forward to supping. The horrid punch at the ball was the only thing she'd had all day. There was more than ample room in the supper box but Cyrus seemed more comfortable standing outside. And an arrogant man like Sloan would never think to invite Cyrus to join them.

When Tess didn't think she could wait any longer, the plates came. She frowned down at the miniscule portions and, with a sigh, carved up her tiny piece of chicken. As she had nothing in common with Sloan, the conversation had dried up quickly. Tess wondered that Lady Stadwell could even eat considering how tight and pursed her lips were. Every time Sloan's attention was diverted, Lady Stadwell would shoot him a killing glance. Her glares were in stark contrast to the joyous expressions depicted on the mural behind her head.

Completely oblivious, Sloan swirled the arrack in his glass. Glimmering lights reflected in the liquor. "What an outrageous price for such measly fare," he said with a disdainful sniff.

A constant flow of patrons paraded by their table. Tess entertained herself by people-watching and remarked a particularly odd-looking character with striped breeches and a pointed beard stroll past. When he sauntered by a fourth time, Tess was certain it was not just by coincidence.

Confirming her suspicions, when the man stopped to check his watch in front of their box, Sloan sat up straight and plunked his goblet down. "I know the perfect location to view the fireworks. But we must be quick about it."

Lady Stadwell, obviously exhausted from the long evening, leaned heavily upon Cyrus. Sloan did not offer his arm, and Tess hurried to keep up with his rapid pace. A thrill ran through her. This might very well be the opportunity she was waiting for.

It was a swift exchange. If Tess had blinked she would have missed it. The bearded man approached. His pace matched Sloan's. The men made a show of clashing shoulders. "Sorry, old man, my clumsiness," Sloan said, and an envelope switched hands. With one motion, Sloan tucked it into his waistcoat. Instantly, his pace slowed and he was soon walking side by side with Tess.

"It seems Lady Stadwell's spirit is flagging," Tess remarked.

Sloan shot a glance over his shoulder. "Perhaps we shall save the fireworks for another evening."

To which Tess readily agreed.

Sloan maneuvered the party down the Grand Walk toward the gates. Tess listened for the next boom of rockets. When they sounded, she swiveled on her heels and clutched his lapels with a cry of surprise. Raising herself on tiptoes, she lifted her lips to his. A shower of light lit up the sky overhead. He did not react instantly. He seemed stunned by her brazenness. Finally, he dipped his head and she curled her hand around the nape of his neck with one hand and plucked the package from his waistcoat with the other. She enfolded it in her palm and took an awkward step back. It was done so quickly that she had only time to think of the kiss after it had happened. Disgust shivered up her back. There was no denying he was a well-made man: tall, blond and elegantly proportioned. But Tess likened the experience to kissing a worm.

"I wish they'd shot those fireworks off earlier." With a self-satisfied smile, Sloan snatched up her hand and tugged her down a passage toward a dim, wooded area.

Stopping just out of Cyrus's range of vision, Sloan patted his coat as though checking pockets. And here she thought she'd been so clever. Her heart rate quickened and her mouth grew suddenly dry. She crushed the package in her hand and prepared to flee straight into Cyrus's massive arms.

Surprisingly, Sloan's hand did not come up empty. He unwrapped a piece of cloth, and Tess could just make out the silhouette of a ring. Discreetly, she slipped the package she'd stolen into her pelisse pocket.

"I know this is rather sudden. But the affection you just demonstrated has given me hope that I will not be rebuffed. Miss Starling, would you consent to being my bride?"

Relieved that he hadn't noticed her sleight of hand, she accepted the ring from him without thinking.

"You've no family, correct? Need I obtain approval from your chaperone? Because in truth Lady Stadwell scares the wits from me. Her behavior has been less than friendly. It's as though she harbors some ill will toward me. "

Because of the darkness, Tess could only picture him saying the latter with an unholy smile. Surely he'd guessed why Lady Stadwell disdained him. Or was that part of his unscrupulous nature? To forget completely the victims of his schemes? Certainly, Tess had never sensed any discomfort on his part when there was mention of her father.

As Tess formulated an answer, she felt him shift nearer as though impatient for a response. "Yes, I'm afraid you must speak with her. But please do not broach the subject tonight. Lady Stadwell is weary." Her hands were shaking and she told herself to calm down. This was, after all, an act, and a wedding would never take place.

In a daze, she let him guide her back to the lit path where Cyrus and Lady Stadwell waited.

"Lass, you are making a mistake," Cyrus muttered under his breath.

He couldn't possibly have known about the proposal but the kiss done under the display of lights he likely hadn't missed.

Chapter Thirteen

Tess muffled a yawn with her gloved hand as she approached the gleaming coach. What she wouldn't give for a night spent at home. Cyrus tossed his cigar aside and straightened his coat before handing Lady Stadwell up into the carriage. Tess, her hand completely lost in his meaty paw, heard his clucking tongue. The man was still scolding her for the insignificant peck she'd planted on Sloan. The carriage jounced under his weight as he hauled himself onto the box to sit beside the coachman. Suspiciously, since Lord Marcliffe's arrival, Cyrus had accompanied them everywhere. Even when they'd taken a short stroll in the park, he had followed like a hulking shadow.

"Dreary night. A play would have at least been more engaging than the opera," Lady Stadwell said. "Besides we are wasting our time with these assignations with that horrid man. We should be finding you a suitable husband."

"It is hardly an assignation. 'Twill be a cordial visit."

"You do not suppose, my dear, that I missed that kiss at Vauxhall." They had not lit the interior lamp, so Tess could only imagine Lady Stadwell's disapproving frown.

"I do have an excuse for my behavior. The kiss was a diversion. I spied a man handing Sloan a small package. And now I have it in my possession." Tess could not bring herself to mention that she had Sloan's betrothal ring in her possession as well.

"What is it?" Despite Lady Stadwell's obvious displeasure with the way Tess had obtained the package, she could not keep the interest from her voice.

Tess smoothed her satin skirt and with nothing but pallid moonlight to guide her actions, she adjusted her elbow-length kidskin gloves so they scrunched just so at the wrist. "Truthfully, I have not a clue. It looks somewhat like tea, but it has a peculiar scent. Perhaps it is some illicit substance."

"Let us hope," Lady Stadwell said. "Though I am convinced that Sloan is fully aware that his swindle caused my dear husband's apoplexy, he acts as if those blond curls form a halo. How I wish I could slap that revolting smile from his face."

A crush of people thronged the entrance to the opera house. Cyrus signaled that they wait, even going so far as to stand before the coach door making an exit impossible. As the last of the attendees swept into the building, Cyrus allowed them to exit. From the seat, Tess plucked the silk shawl shot through with silver thread.

"You are not wearing that useless thing, are you, my dear?" Lady Stadwell asked.

"It is too lovely. I cannot resist it," Tess replied.

Cyrus escorted them only as far as the doors. Tess tucked Lady Stadwell's hand in her arm as they climbed the stairs to the balcony. They had only just taken their seats in the box when the curtains twitched. Sloan swaggered in. A street ruffian in a gentleman's wardrobe, Tess thought. He bowed his head in Lady Stadwell's direction before giving Tess's gloved fingers a squeeze. He flicked his tailcoats and took the chair beside Tess.

"Looking lovely as usual. You'd look even more so with my ring on your finger. Tonight may afford me the opportunity to ask Lady Stadwell."

Tess managed a smile and a bat of her lashes. "Patience, sir. Her mood this evening is a little glum."

"Oh, pity." Sloan brushed at non-existent lint on his lapel. "Have you had a visit from the illustrious lord of the manor?"

"He has made himself scarce since the night of the Gray's ball." Tess spoke in measured tones hoping to keep the searing disappointment from her voice.

The velvet curtains parted again and a far more welcome figure made his entrance, Captain Gibbs in full dress uniform.

His wiry hair had been tamed for the occasion but a couple of stubborn tufts still stuck up boyishly. His broad grin warmed Tess's heart.

Sloan acknowledged the captain with a lazy nod. He sat at ease, not the least bit ruffled by the captain's presence. Yet when Lord Marcliffe had strode into the ballroom the previous evening, Tess had sensed his agitation. It occurred to her that Lady Stadwell's scheme had really been rather brilliant. She had correctly gauged the character of the enemy. But there had been one small flaw in her thinking. Sloan was not obsessed with both men, but only one man; Lord Marcliffe.

"How ever did you know to find us?" Lady Stadwell asked Captain Gibbs. Evidently, Tess was not the only one who found his sudden appearance suspect.

Captain Gibbs gave a hesitant smile, then, glancing at Tess, responded. "Why, I spotted Miss Starling's famed hair from across the theatre." He moved to stand beside Lady Stadwell's chair. "Miss Starling, are you enjoying the music?"

Tess laughed. "It hasn't started yet, Captain."

This was clearly unfamiliar environs for the captain. Apparently, Lord Marcliffe was enlisting all his friends to keep his aunt safe. Tess moved to the edge of her seat, placed her hand on the railing and peered over the balcony. Her gaze hopped from one tall, dark-haired man to the next.

Sloan propped his chin atop interlocked fingers and turned to stare at her. His eyes were a crystalline blue and they chilled her to the bone. "And who might you be looking for, Miss Starling?" He pulled a pair of opera glasses from his pocket and offered them to her. "Perhaps he will be easier to spot with these."

"Spot whom?" She refused the glasses and settled back in her seat. "I was watching the orchestra tune up."

He slid his eyes sideways, regarding her beneath hooded lids. "I think I shall brave your aunt's temper tonight. For I fear the prize will be snatched from me."

Tess nodded weakly, unable to come up with another excuse for postponing the betrothal announcement. She dreaded to think how Lady Stadwell would take the news and even more so how Lord Marcliffe would receive it. Or perhaps she dreaded more the thought that he would be indifferent to the idea.

The captain cleared his throat. "How are you occupying yourself these days, Sloan?"

He kept his profile to the captain as he spoke. "Dirtying my hands with trade, actually. Overseeing a shipment to China."

Tess became alert. Her lessons with Lydia Midwinter had convinced her that a mistress could coax the information from a man with sweet talk and a talented body. Would any subject be taboo in the bedchamber? Masquerading as a prim daughter of a viscount, all she could do was glean information by paying close attention.

"What type of goods?" the captain asked.

"I've no doubt Lady Stadwell and Miss Starling would prefer

an end to this dull conversation." Sloan flicked the lorgnette handle and opened the spectacles. He scanned the crowd. "That is Jessup across the way, is it not? I imagine that hitch in Marcliffe's step has hobbled him. Such loyal friends to look out for his interests."

Lady Stadwell looked past Tess and aimed a fierce gaze at Sloan, who paid her no mind and continued to study the audience. "He is hardly lame, sir. On most days you would not even notice his injuries," she said.

"My dear lady, do not take me to task. Your nephew is completely admirable."

Lady Stadwell sat back with an indignant rustle of taffeta and Sloan gave Tess a conspirator's wink. "I only wish I could boast of an exemplary war record."

The man was obsessed with Lord Marcliffe. It wasn't only Tess's pedigree that he was interested in, it was her connection, no matter how vague, to Lord Marcliffe.

The orchestra began, the stage curtain drew up and Tess glanced down. Dizziness overtook her. She had to get out of the confines of the box. "Lady Stadwell, you were absolutely right about the shawl. It is completely frivolous. I feel a chill. I am certain I have something warmer in the coach. I shall have Cyrus fetch it for me."

"Child, you did not bring anything else," Lady Stadwell said.

"It's sweltering in here," Sloan said dismissively.

Tess ignored him and stood on wobbly legs. "I am certain I left my pelisse in the carriage after our walk in the park."

With an audible sigh, Sloan got to his feet.

"You will miss the opening." Lady Stadwell began untying the ribbon of her mantle. "Take mine. I am perfectly warm.

"Most definitely not. Now do not fret. I will be back shortly."

Thankfully, Sloan kept his negligent stance. He did not seem in any hurry to act the escort or offer to get the coat himself.

Tess placed a restraining hand on the captain's arm as he made a move to follow her through the curtains. "No, please. I will not have anyone miss a minute of the music because of my vanity."

There was an attendant at the entrance whom Tess instructed to give her regrets to the occupants of the loge, to explain to them that she was suffering a headache. Outside, she spied Cyrus in conversation with John, the coachman. Tess draped the shawl over her hair and hurried to the other side of the road. She peeked behind to find Cyrus in pursuit.

"No need to worry, Lady Stadwell is perfectly safe with Captain Gibbs." She tossed the words back at him as she hurried her step. Who would have thought such a big man could move so swiftly? It occurred to Tess suddenly that not only was Lord Marcliffe protecting his aunt, but he was keeping Tess on a restrictive leash.

Tess weaved between parked coaches, through tight, dangerous spots that brought her too close to the harnessed horses. She knew Cyrus's bulk would not allow him to follow.

A shabby rented carriage stood in an alleyway. With a frantic wave, she hailed the driver and he tipped his hat at her approach. She rattled off the address of the townhouse as she boarded. Tess sat back against the cracked leather cushions and smiled to herself.

Tess knew she faced one more obstacle before she could enjoy a few moments of peace. Predictably, Jane came running the instant Tess entered the townhouse. The maid was always ready to pounce, far too helpful in Tess's estimation.

"Jane, you have uncanny hearing," she said with frustration.

Jane smiled as if it were a compliment and pursued Tess up to the bedchamber. "You've come home alone, my lady? If you don't mind me saying so, he's a handsome one."

"Who?"

"Mr. Sloan, of course." Jane hung up the dress and with deliberation smoothed out the wrinkles. Next, she concentrated on laying out Tess's gloves, lining them up precisely in the wardrobe drawer.

"Please leave that be and help me out of my stays." When the undergarment was finally loosened, Tess yanked it off and threw it atop the chair.

Jane picked up the silver-backed brush from the bed stand. "Shall I brush your hair out, my lady?"

Tess snatched it from her. "Please, I have been fretted over by mother hens all night."

Jane looked stricken. She curtsied and shuffled out.

Finally alone, Tess plucked the pins from her hair and shook out her mane of curls. She threw herself atop the bed and lifted her heavy hair so that it cascaded over the pillow. The linen felt deliciously cool against her nape.

Tess sat up to pull the sheet over her bare legs. "Oh, damn," she cried as her hair snagged on the ornate ironwork of the headboard. Blast Lydia Midwinter and her absurd bed. For a part of this wretched evening, she'd managed to escape Sloan, Lady Stadwell and even her dogged protector, Cyrus, at the theatre. Now she was caught fast by the diabolical bed. It seemed even inanimate objects were conspiring to remind her that she'd forfeited her freedom for the pursuit of revenge.

Wincing, she twisted around to get a better view. Her cry,

which had not been particularly loud, brought the sound of boots thundering up the stairs. The heavy footsteps could only belong to Cyrus. Naturally he'd followed her home, she thought with irritation. In this most compromising position, on all fours with only the thin chemise covering her bottom, she yanked furiously on her hair, only to tangle it more.

"Cyrus, stay right where you are," she ordered. The footsteps were just outside her door. "Cyrus, I shall have your head if you step one foot in this room." She heard the click of the latch. "For God's sake, I am not decent!"

She felt the breeze whisper over her bare legs as the door swung open then shut. "From this vantage point, I'd say you are quite plainly more than decent." She gasped at the drawling, familiar voice. If she turned her head to look at Lord Marcliffe, she risked pulling an entire hank of hair out along with the scalp it was attached to. She had no choice but to remain in this humiliating position. His breathing sounded ragged as he placed his candle on the bedside table.

"What the devil are you doing here?"

"That's the gratitude I get. Cyrus came to the club, worried because you'd raced home from the theatre. I was concerned."

"Cyrus, I assume, was stationed outside the building shadowing my every move. My very own bodyguard. And I assume Jane is in your employ because she is always watching me, as well." She stopped struggling with her hair for a moment and twisted her face enough to see him.

"Cyrus, yes. Jane's curiosity I take no credit for."

"Do you take no credit for Gibbs and Jessup, as well?"

"You might say they are lending me a hand." His mouth tilted into a crooked, cocky smile. "So, rabbit, what were you running from?"

She knew he expected her to admit she was escaping

149

Sloan, but she wouldn't give him the satisfaction. "The theatre was stifling, overheated. I stepped out for some air and, on impulse, hired a cab. I did have a message delivered to your aunt and Sloan explaining that I had a headache. I do hope Sloan won't be terribly angry."

"How thoughtful of you to be so concerned about Sloan's feelings," he said, his tone thick with sarcasm. "You never give me the same consideration."

"So punish me," she dared him.

He took her words as an invitation and shoved the hem of her chemise up over her hips so that her naked bottom was exposed to him. He groaned as his hand slid up the inside of her thigh. His fingers flicked over the moist, pink folds of her quim. She was convinced he was purposely teasing her. She wanted him so badly. Gripping the headboard with her hands, she parted her knees and tilted her bottom upward, offering it to him. In return, he delivered a solid slap to her backside.

"Oh," she said, surprised mostly by the fact that she enjoyed it. She could feel the heat from his handprint and she itched for more. He forced her knees farther apart just before his big hand delivered another punishing slap. He'd positioned his hand in such a way that his fingers struck her quim, leaving a stinging, delicious ache. Her bottom felt hot, and she was sure it was quite red.

"That's enough," she said, out of pure frustration. She wanted him inside of her. Wanted him to thrust hard and deep as he spanked her. But she would not beg.

He flung himself down on the bed. The mattress dipped under his weight. He stretched out his legs and leaned back against the headboard. She was happy to see the frustrated sulk on his lips. He made no move to disentangle her hair. Instead, he scrutinized every visible inch of her. His lips kicked up into a nasty smile.

"Damn, but you are glorious from every angle." He was near enough for her to taste the whiskey on his breath.

Unshaven, his black hair overlong, he looked nothing like a peer of the realm. More like a brigand, she thought, as she glimpsed the pistol tucked in his waistband.

"Why are you armed?" she asked.

"Cyrus said you nearly got yourself killed diving between the carriages. I thought you might be in trouble."

She tugged the hair that anchored her to the bed. "I am in trouble. Hand me some scissors, so I can cut myself free."

"Not a chance."

"This bed is miserable. It is the second time this week I've snagged my hair on it."

"I'm only sorry I missed it the first time," he said with a chuckle and turned onto his side, his shoulder nestled against her breast. Her nipple tightened at the feel of him. He stiffened. She knew he'd felt her reaction to him. "Christ," he muttered, and she felt a slight tremor run through his body.

He seemed to be able to see better in this half-light than she, and his deft fingers soon had her freed. She crawled hurriedly off the bed and covered herself with a quilt.

"I've something to show you." She removed the paper-wrapped item from the dressing table by the bed. "Sloan has said he intends to sell tea to China."

Lord Marcliffe laughed. "Tea?" He heaved himself off the bed.

"I thought it ridiculous myself. And then I happened upon this." She handed him the small parcel.

"Just happened upon this, did you?"

"Well, actually, I snatched it from the underbrush where

he'd discarded it."

He raised a black brow in question.

"He'd taken me to the gardens one night. As the fireworks were thundering, a man approached. I'm not certain there was even a word exchanged between him and Sloan. But that little package did pass between them."

A muscle in his jaw flexed. "You went to Vauxhall alone with Sloan?"

"Of course not. In truth, it was your aunt who occupied Sloan's attention for a moment while I retrieved that. It doesn't smell much like tea, does it?"

He whistled thinly through his teeth. "Such sweet lips, such an outrageous lie. How did you really come by this packet?"

She shrugged, pretending nonchalance, but she intertwined her fingers to stop them from trembling. "I lifted it from his pocket, like a regular cutpurse."

"While my aunt distracted him?" His skeptical brow lifted higher. "She has far more skill in espionage than I would have credited. I will have to congratulate her."

"Aggravating man." She snatched a pillow from the bed and smacked him with it. He tugged it easily out of her grasp and tossed it aside.

"Tell me what really happened."

She sighed heavily. "Obviously I'm a far better pickpocket than a liar. Your aunt had nothing to do with it. I was the distraction," she said. "There were fireworks and I pretended to be startled by the bang." Suddenly, she gasped as though startled and clutched at Tallon. His eyes narrowed with distrust as she rose up on tiptoes. He was far taller than Sloan, so she wrapped one hand around his neck and tugged his face closer.

"And I kissed him," she said against his mouth, her lips so close they brushed his. She could feel his neck tense beneath her fingers. Immediately, she released her hold on him and took a step back. She showed him the watch she'd plucked from his pocket. It was still attached by a chain to his waistcoat. Her fingers had not been clever enough to unhook the latch.

She shrugged and tucked it back in his pocket.

"Damn it." He peeled open a corner of the package and a peculiar exotic aroma settled in the air between them. "Opium," he said. He'd identified the substance too quickly in her estimation. Another sign that he'd experienced much of the dark, seamier side of life. "And Sloan intends to sell this in China. Sloan has always had a fascination with such substances." He shoved the package into his coat pocket. "Have you sampled any of Sloan's elixirs?"

"The ones that make a woman beg for a man to—to—"

"To fuck her. Yes, those."

She could feel the scarlet heat rise in her cheeks. "You cannot be serious. Your aunt accompanies me everywhere."

"Smart woman, my aunt."

He snatched up his candlestick, sending something clinking to the floor. Hunkering down on his heels, he cast the light over the floor. The object caught the light, and the crystalline facets winked up at them. He scooped it up.

"What's this?" Standing, he bounced the ring off the palm of his hand.

"A ring."

"Yes, I gathered as much. Who gave it to you?"

"Sloan, of course," she said, hoping to sound offhand.

His lashes dropped, and he studied what he held. "Why, Tess?"

"It's the silliest thing—really." She hesitated, nibbling her bottom lip nervously.

He glared at her. His eyes appeared midnight blue in the murky light.

"Sloan has proposed," Tess said weakly.

He moved to the window and threw open the sash. Ice-cold air swept into the room, and Tess hugged the quilt around her. He stuck his hand outside, the extravagant ring merely resting on his palm. She knew without a doubt he'd have no qualms about turning his hand over and letting it drop to the brick courtyard. "Proposed what?" he asked.

"Marriage."

"And you have accepted?"

She nodded.

He tilted back his head and looked at her suspiciously through slitted eyes. "You have no dowry, and Sloan is venal. What have you done to deserve this?" He slanted his hand so the ring slid an inch nearer to the ground.

Tess moved cautiously toward him, afraid that a sudden move might prompt him to drop the ring. She grabbed his arm with both hands, and the quilt fell away, puddling around her bare feet. His muscles were formidable, and she knew she didn't have a prayer. But she wasn't about to let him throw away her one chance at destroying Sloan.

"I don't understand why you are so resentful. How can this not be a good thing? Isn't this what your aunt wanted? I have the opportunity to find out exactly what he's up to." She felt his arm shake with anger beneath her fingers. Dropping her hold on him, she backed up a step.

The panes rattled as he closed the window with a bang. He took her hand and dropped the ring into it. "A truly cunning little thing. You refuse my proposal but accept my enemy's."

"He is my enemy, as well. Do you really think I can be bought with trinkets like this?"

She took a few tentative steps in his direction. He wrapped his hand around her arm, and, applying pressure, brought her to her knees before him.

"Convince me."

In that position, it was instantly apparent what he wanted from her. Lady Stadwell had warned her that despite expensive clothes and arrogant manners, aristocrats were the same as any man, beasts at heart. Tess had to admit that she was especially fond of this feral side of Lord Marcliffe. He removed his pistol and placed it on the dresser. After tossing his coat aside, he pushed the braces off his shoulders.

With unsteady hands, she lowered his trousers. She fumbled with the ribbon of his drawers. She couldn't believe how desperately she wanted to touch him. His fingers dug into her thick hair, and he tugged her upward. She resisted, remaining on her knees.

"Forget it," he spat out. "It is apparent how distasteful a thing this is for you. A fine display of martyrdom, that."

Clearly, he'd mistaken her nervousness for reluctance. "I want this as much as you."

With the ribbon untied, she pulled down his drawers. His anger had not softened his needs. When she released his shaft, it sprang hugely hard and erect before her. Her tongue flicked the slit at the tip. He leaned over and took a fistful of her chemise. She lifted her arms so he could draw it over her head. Kneeling naked at his feet, she curled her small hand around him and was rewarded with a groan of pleasure. How, she wondered, did women manage this feat? Though he was surely bigger than most.

Her lips, cold and certainly turning a shade of blue from the frigid air still hovering in the room, melted and molded around the heat of him. His body jolted as her teeth scraped lightly over him. That clumsiness had certainly proved her a novice. She would have to do better than that and soon found that love heightened one's instincts. She cupped the sacs between his thighs. They felt luxuriously heavy in her hand. And then she took turns cradling each of his balls in her mouth. Using her tongue, she tasted them eagerly.

His thighs trembled beneath her hands. "Look at me," he demanded, his voice gruff.

The candle had been extinguished by the flood of night air. The half-moon glazed the room in pale silver. She sat back a little on her heels, and after putting the fleshy head of his cock in her mouth to suck, she lifted her eyes. He craned his neck forward as though searching her face. His hair draped his features, making the glint of his eyes the only thing visible. If that was all she could see in this dim light, then plainly he could not see the adoration in her eyes. And she was glad of it. She had no wish to hand the man her heart on a silver platter.

His big hand cupped the back of her head, pressing her to take more of him. "Relax, sweeting." Remembering Miss Midwinter's instructions, she loosened her throat. She gripped his buttocks, her fingers digging into his taut muscles. He thrust forward, guiding his cock deeper.

"Tess, do you want more?"

Moaning, she clutched him closer, wanting to devour all of him.

"What a beautiful, greedy little mouth you have," he said, his voice raw with desire. He stroked even deeper. She could feel him at the back of her throat now.

She began working her mouth up and down the hardened

length of him. And then his hands tightened on her head, stilling her movements. With smooth, delicious thrusts he took possession of her mouth and her senses. Her quim tingled with heat. She was close to climaxing from servicing him. Astonishingly, she enjoyed being used by him this way.

Tess could feel his body tense, and he gave a gallant effort to bring her to her feet. But she clung to him tighter, wanting to enjoy every last bit of the experience. She swallowed as much as her mouth would hold, but a little of the cream spilled from her lips. Getting to her feet, she wiped the cream from her chin and licked it from her fingers.

He stared at her as he buttoned his trousers. He was looking at her as he had when she'd stripped off her frumpy disguise, as though he were seeing her anew. She felt like an exotic creature beneath his half-lidded scrutiny.

"That was your first time." There was not a note of doubt in the statement.

It was not the reaction she was expecting. She plucked her chemise from the ground and slipped it on. "Was I terribly inept?"

Dead silence greeted her embarrassing question. She bit her lip to stop it from quivering.

Finally he spoke, his voice sounding huskier than usual. "You are..." There was a nightmarish pause. "...a very fast learner."

She exhaled a shivering breath. *A fast learner.* That was all he had to say to her. But what had she expected from a man as hard as Lord Marcliffe? Words of love?

He sat at the edge of the bed and began pulling off his boot. He was intending to stay the night.

"Lady Stadwell will be returning from the theatre soon."

One big black boot dropped to the floor. "My aunt goes straight to bed after a night in town. And I will be out before dawn." The second boot dropped.

There was a scratching noise at the door. Tess quickly snatched up her heavy cashmere shawl and whipped it around her shoulders, ever conscious of the unpredictable man on her bed.

She shook her head frantically when he got to his feet. "Stay there," she implored. "It is only Jane."

She cracked open the door, letting a sliver of the hall lamplight in, and peered out at Jane.

"Mr. Sloan has brought your aunt home. He's asked to see you."

"William is here in the house?"

"Not in the house, no. Cyrus made him wait on the stoop. And he isn't happy about it. Not at all." Jane stretched her neck, apparently hoping to see what Tess was hiding.

"You must send him away. Tell him I am sleeping."

"Yes, miss. If he proves stubborn, I'm sure Cyrus can convince him to leave."

Tess shut the door, thinking her night would have been far simpler if she'd just remained at the theatre. Not as exciting, though. She could still taste him. A delicious shiver ran through her. She turned to look at him. He was retrieving his pistol. The moonlight glanced dully off the pearl handle.

"For me, it is 'my lord this' and 'my lord that'. But that criminal, you call by his given name. And you refuse me, but you kiss him," Lord Marcliffe observed.

The nerve of the man, assuming a proprietary right to her lips even though he didn't care for kissing. "It was nothing but a peck. I'm completely innocent." She hesitated for a moment.

"Well, mostly innocent."

His expression darkened forbiddingly and she hurried to explain herself. "I did something that I am ashamed of."

He took an intimidating step toward her.

Realizing it was like stopping an angry bull with a handkerchief, she put up her hand to hold him back. "I'm not talking about *that*. I spoke against your character to win Sloan's approval. And I've felt wretched about it ever since."

He grabbed his boots. "Pray, don't lose any sleep over it." Before exiting, he made certain no prying servants lingered in the hallway. With a curse, he shut the door behind him.

ಬ

The next morning, peering in the mirror, Tess noted the dark rings under her eyes, courtesy of one Lord Marcliffe.

She found him downstairs in the library asleep in the most awkward position. His long legs, complete with boots, dangled over the arm of the settee. Scrunched forward, his chin digging into his chest, he looked thoroughly uncomfortable, and it gladdened her heart. She fought the urge to hurl a book at his black head.

With mischief on her mind, she headed down the servants' steps to the basement. Once in the kitchen, she purposely clanged the iron brazier atop the stove, and even though she was expecting it, the jarring metallic sound made her jump. Then she filled the teakettle and banged it down hard on the stove.

All her good work had served its purpose, she thought, when he shuffled into the kitchen.

His eyes narrowed at the sight of her. "I can hear your

bloody cooking upstairs," he growled, pressing his temples with his forefingers. "My God, woman, you torture me in my dreams and in my waking hours."

"Oh really? I am in your dreams, am I?" She tried not to sound too pleased with the notion.

He walked up so close, she could see the dark stubble on his chin. "Apparently, you missed the key word: *torture.*" He touched her bottom lip with his finger and tugged it lightly downward. "A man does not sleep easily after lips like these have been wrapped around his cock."

Tess returned her attention to the stove so he wouldn't see the color creeping up her cheeks. She set the kettle to light and reminded herself to breathe.

"Why isn't the cook doing that?" he asked.

"You know I enjoy baking." Her hands shook as she scooped the flour, half of which ended up powdering the front of her skirt. She could feel the heat of his gaze on her back. She prayed that the civilized side of his character would assert itself and he wouldn't mention her lovemaking skills again.

They both turned at the sound of Jane's twittering laugh.

"What a mess you're making, Miss Starling. Here, let me do that." They had a bit of a tug of war with the spoon before Tess relented.

"Jane, please bring the tea up when it's ready," Tess said and followed Lord Marcliffe up the stairs.

Tess had just settled onto a dining room chair when the doorknocker banged. She flinched, knowing very well who it might be.

"My, but you are jumpy little rabbit. Would that be your betrothed? Christ, it's hardly daybreak," he said, and stalked toward the entry.

With a hurried step, she moved to bar his way.

"Move aside. I'm going to wring someone's neck," he stated.

There was a glint of violence in his eyes. With her hands flat on his chest, she looked up at him. "Listen," she hissed, "I have worked too hard to let you ruin this."

"I wouldn't want to destroy your damn scheme." But he wouldn't budge from the center of the dining room.

A servant opened the door and was nearly trampled by two men bearing baskets of white flowers. The servant directed them through the entrance hall to the dining room. Tess plastered herself against the wall and watched in stunned silence as the men made trip after trip to the street returning with ever bigger, more ostentatious arrays of blossoms. She did not have the courage to look in Lord Marcliffe's direction to gauge his reaction. When they were at last finished, there was not a surface bare of flowers in the room. She leaned over and buried her face in a bouquet of white roses tied with hyssop and southernwood. The scent reminded her of her country garden.

"One more thing, miss," the last of the men said as he was leaving. He pulled from his pocket what looked like a fur ball.

The fur ball yipped. She took the puppy from the man's grimy hands. "Thank you," she said with a smile.

"'Tis I who should be doing the thanking, miss. Your admirer bought out my entire cart." He pulled a wad of banknotes from his pocket and riffled the edges with his thumb. "Generous fellow."

"I'll trade you one of those pound notes for three guineas," Lord Marcliffe offered.

Tess turned to see Lord Marcliffe striding toward them, knocking the petals off the flowers on the mantel with his broad shoulders. A couple of petals caught in his long, shaggy hair. She giggled at the sight of him. He scowled in return.

161

Lord Marcliffe handed the flower seller the gold coins.

"That's a handsome exchange." The man peeled off a bill and eagerly gave it to the earl. He wrapped his fist around the coins. "I can keep a confidence, that's for certain." The man glanced meaningfully from Lord Marcliffe to Tess.

Tess found Lord Marcliffe's gesture suspect. Had the money been meant as a gratuity or as a means to keep the man silent? And why did he ask for a pound note in exchange?

She watched him tuck the banknote into his waistcoat pocket.

"What is that—a rat?" he asked, directing his gaze to the small bundle she held.

"It's an adorable puppy." She rubbed her face in the snow white fur.

"I wouldn't think you would be so easily won over."

Too much stimulation and not enough sleep were making her feel giddy. "You must admit, it is beautiful." She spun around, letting her fingers skim the flowers. "It makes me wonder if I couldn't just get him to ruin himself by spending like a madman."

His scowl deepened. "The thief's amassed a fortune. A pretty smile may have gotten you this wagonload of flowers, but imagine what you will have to do to bankrupt him."

"Must you always be so cruel to me? You are only angry because my plan is working."

"Your plan is heading into very dangerous territory. And without me, you will eventually find yourself unhappily wed to the bastard."

"Well then, I do hope you find something out soon so that I may end this alliance," she said.

"So, despite the gifts, you are still disenchanted with

Sloan?"

"I was speaking of this alliance." She used her forefinger to gesture between Lord Marcliffe and herself.

With one sweep of his arm he cleared the entire mantel of vases. The crash was tremendous.

The scared puppy nearly leapt from her arms and she clutched it tighter to her chest. It was her fault. Why was she always goading him? Hearing the servants on the stairs she spoke quickly. "That was a ridiculous thing to say and there's no truth to it."

"Then give Sloan back the ring," he said.

"You know I can't do that."

"How long do you think I'm going to be satisfied with the crumbs of passion you toss my way? I want full possession of you and nothing less will do."

He'd finally admitted it. It was lust driving him and not affection, as she'd hoped. How she wished her heart was as indifferent to him.

"All your want of me would be more believable if it hadn't taken you two weeks to get to London."

"Actually, two weeks and two days," he corrected. "Your father's finances were in a greater state of disarray than I had anticipated."

"My father's finances? I don't understand."

"His debts are cleared now," he said.

His forbidding look warned her that she dare not thank him. But she had to wonder what he expected in payment. Suddenly she needed air. She stepped over the broken glass and fled with the dog into the garden.

Chapter Fourteen

Lord Marcliffe returned to his club, but his surrogate remained. Tess looked across the room at Cyrus who was leisurely paging through a book as though the library was one of his usual destinations. Constantly attended to, she felt like a child on leading strings. After several minutes, Cyrus's head fell forward and his heavy snores soon made it impossible to read. Tess set her book aside. Not that she could concentrate anyway. She kept reliving her last conversation with Lord Marcliffe. Knowing he only wanted her to fulfill his needs did not lessen the ache she felt in his absence.

Jane stuck her head in the doorway and motioned silently so as not to rouse Cyrus.

Once Tess was in the hallway, Jane kept her voice low. "I heard your little dog barking in the garden. I hope there's nothing wrong."

Tess draped her shawl over her shoulders and followed Jane.

"'Tis a shame about all those flowers," Jane said with a sideways glance.

Tess ignored the comment and, leaving the prying maid behind, hurried out into the dark yard. There was no sound or sight of the new pup. She clapped her hands and moved deeper into the garden. "Flurry, where are you?"

From behind, she felt the sudden warmth and presence of someone. It was as though her wishes had made Lord Marcliffe appear. His arm snaked around her waist. The scent of sandalwood enveloped her.

"Tallon," she said, and pressed her head back against his chest. The arm tightened immediately around her waist, and she knew in an instant she'd made a terrible mistake.

"I wanted to surprise you and I'm the one surprised. How interesting that you mistook my hands for his. I didn't know we had so much in common."

"William, you are jumping to conclusions. I've never even kissed the man," she said, her voice quavering.

"Don't trouble yourself. You've only confirmed my suspicions." He rubbed his body against her. "I doubt any woman would decline a proposition from Lord Marcliffe." Sloan pushed her head roughly to the side and his mouth clamped down on her throat. He punished her with hard, bruising kisses, his teeth scraping her skin. She gasped.

"My ship will be ready to sail earlier than expected. In a month's time, we will take a coach to Gretna Green and from there to port."

She struggled to pull away, and his grip tightened, squeezing the breath from her. "You would not like to see me challenge your dear friend, the earl. You may think him a better shot. After all, he was a soldier. But he hasn't my cunning. I can make situations bend in my favor. So it's best, you see, not to purr the man's name like that."

He gave her a brutal squeeze and she felt as if her ribs might break. And then he released her and slithered back into the shadows.

A tug at her skirt made her jump. A little white ball of fur stared up at her. She lifted the dog into her arms and buried her face in its fur.

She was certain Sloan would arrange murder rather than face Lord Marcliffe on a dueling field. She had wanted to entrap Sloan, but now she was the one caught in the snare.

∞

The next day, Tess convinced Lady Stadwell to take some fresh air with her. But the afternoon in the park did not sweep the terrifying encounter with Sloan from Tess's mind. Having little appetite, she skipped dinner and retired early. She found the monstrous headboard with the wrought iron ornamentation gone. In its place stood a sleek, cherrywood bed. She wondered if she imagined it, but the bed seemed peculiarly sized, as though it had been built especially for the man who'd purchased it. Suspiciously longer than normal, it would hold a man as tall as Tallon comfortably. But the width was narrow. Two people lying side by side would have to sleep very close. She envisioned his long body curled around hers and thrilled at the notion.

Then she had a very different vision of Sloan occupying that same bed. She imagined herself crushed against the wall to avoid him. The thought made her want to retch. She couldn't leave the room fast enough, nearly tripping down the stairs in an effort to distance herself from the disturbing idea.

The parlor fire had long since died away and Lady Stadwell had gone off to bed. Tess wrapped her heavy shawl around her shoulders and took a seat before the cold hearth. She heard heavy footsteps and frowned with frustration knowing that Cyrus would soon invade her solitude.

"Cyrus, I'm perfectly fine. You need not..." She sighed with pleasure at the sight of Lord Marcliffe. He looked disturbingly handsome in his stark black attire.

He strode to the hearth, hunkered down on his haunches and proceeded to build a fire.

Her delight in seeing him quickly devolved to worry. She was certain that Sloan was not only watching the house but contemplating a murderous deed against the man she loved. Knowing too well that Lord Marcliffe would misinterpret her concern, she still needed to ask, "If Sloan finds out about your late night visitations, what then?"

The moment he sat down, Flurry leapt onto his lap. He ruffled the dog's fur. "Do you think I care a damn?"

She'd half expected his answer. There was nothing she could say to warn him off. The man was too mule-headed. "What's come of the packet of opium?" she asked hopefully.

"He's purchasing the narcotic from Turkey. Plans on smuggling it into China."

"Smuggling? There must be some penalty for that." She could not curb the eagerness in her voice. If Sloan were imprisoned then Lord Marcliffe would not be harmed.

"Sorry to disappoint you, my little trickster, but it's done all the time. The fact that opium trade has been outlawed in China means nothing. He will simply conceal the contraband with legal cargo. Then all he needs to do is pay squeeze money to the opium buyers who pass it along to the Chinese officials." The puppy was now sleeping in the crook of his arm.

"Whiskey?" he asked hopefully.

"We have some sherry, I believe." That offer did not please him. She felt inadequate. With certainty, his mistress had the cupboard stocked with the things he enjoyed.

"An American is financing the entire venture. Sloan will be sailing under the company's banner. This way he won't risk the ire of the East India Company, which owns the English opium trade. It is possible that the American will never see his boat again. But you cannot imprison someone on a supposition."

Tess felt defeated. It seemed a bleak future with Sloan was assured. Tess got up and walked over to the cigar box. She handed him a cigar and moved a lit candlestick within reach.

His dark blue eyes assessed her. He seemed surprised by the gesture. Dipping his head to the candle flame, he lit the cigar carefully so as not to disturb the puppy. She watched mesmerized as the smoke streamed from his firm lips.

"By the look on your face, one would think that you are anxious to be done with this thing," he said.

"Don't toy with me. You know I'm terrified that this might go on too long." She reached over and swirled her fingers in the white fur on the puppy's head.

"There is another business Sloan might be involved in." He dug into his pocket then tossed a folded banknote onto her lap. "Do you remember when I traded for that?"

She nodded.

"For a closefisted bastard, he was oddly generous with that flower seller. Take a close look. That note is counterfeit."

She inspected it carefully, but found nothing obvious.

He sat forward and pointed out the discrepancy in the design of the Bank of England seal. "The engraver did a near perfect job. But I've had experts confirm it for me."

"Is this enough to put him in gaol?"

"This is a hanging offense. Unfortunately, this single banknote is not enough to convict him." He plucked the banknote from her fingers. "I suggest you break the betrothal before you find your reputation tainted by his criminal acts."

"What? And give up the opportunity of discovering more of

these notes?" She made a grab for it, but he held it just out of reach.

"A moment ago you said you were terrified."

"Well, I am. But my desire for revenge trumps any fears I might have." Tess marveled at how convincing she sounded, since destroying Sloan was no longer a motive. Once she'd realized her own stubbornness had put Lord Marcliffe at risk, revenge had become meaningless. She flashed one of the smiles that always managed to soften his mood. It worked. He reached over and lightly stroked her cheek.

"Stubborn chit. Play this game too long and you might find yourself not only sharing his bed but the scaffold as well."

The softening effect had worn off sooner than she'd expected. "I may have played too long already." She forced a laugh. "We are to be married in a month."

He set the dog down and leaned forward, his arms resting on his spread thighs. "In a month. Well isn't that fucking lovely?"

"We are to be married at Gretna Green. Then we will take the carriage back to his cottage and set sail when the boat is ready."

"A fucking lovely marriage and a fucking lovely honeymoon in a fucking lovely cottage. How sweet." He stood abruptly and stalked over to the glass-fronted cabinet. He swung the door wide, cracking it against the wall, causing a forked fissure in the pane. He stared inside.

"You'll find nothing stronger than sherry."

He paced angrily across the room before turning around and facing her. There was a look in his eyes she'd never seen before. "Terrified. Bollocks! You seem altogether too pleased with the notion. Perhaps you've fallen for that criminal. The man who caused your father's death." He flung his cigar into

169

the hearth and gripped the mantel. Holding himself rigid, his knuckles whitening, he stared into the flames. "I'm sorry, that was cruel."

She could easily forgive his harsh words because he looked so miserable.

He turned to her. "I ask one favor of you. Don't do anything rash until you hear from me again."

Tess nodded, but knew she'd lost control of the situation, and that Sloan might, at anytime, follow through with his threat.

⁗℃

Shadowed by the rotting eaves of an abandoned storefront, Tallon thumbed back the brim of his hat and surveyed his surroundings. The bleak view fit his mood perfectly, the crumbling buildings with their nearly opaque, soot-encrusted windows and the crooked street reeking of gin and offal.

Tallon spotted Gibbs alighting from a hackney coach and stepped out to greet him.

Gibbs jerked back a step. "Must you lurk like that? You frightened the holy hell out of me. By God, Cliffe, it doesn't take much to turn you into a villainous-looking scoundrel—change of clothes and you've arrived."

"At least I don't look like a pigeon plump for the taking. I told you to wear something tattered and old."

Indignant, Gibbs peered down at his lightly smudged olive-colored morning coat and nankeen pantaloons. "This is the shabbiest clothing I own."

Tallon pulled the pistol from the deep pocket of the ancient coat and handed it to Gibbs. "Since you are dressed like that

170

you had better carry the weapon."

Gibbs glanced down at the gun in his hand. "This gets more and more intriguing. Are you going to share with me the purpose of this secret outing?"

"Sloan has stopped throwing the banknotes around. Perhaps he doesn't want to risk gaol just when he is about to embark on a profitable smuggling venture. I'm guessing the greedy bastard has a stack of the fake money lying around in the office he rents here."

Gibbs surveyed the dilapidated building. "Elegant address he's chosen. What merchant would discuss matters with him here?"

"Do remember the type of business that Sloan conducts."

"Will we break into his home next?" Gibbs asked dryly.

"I already know there's nothing there. Jessup scoured his house, as well as the cottage he keeps in Woolwich by the dockyard." He'd spat out the word cottage and fancied himself burning the thing to the ground.

"Do you have the entire battalion working for you? First Cyrus and now Jessup. Gladdens my heart though that Jessup had to suffer through that bloody bore of an opera, too. Couldn't happen to a more deserving fellow." Gibbs combed his hand through his wiry hair, making it stand in spikes.

"I need to find something on Sloan. I feel Tess is in danger."

"Ah, Tess. That is what this harebrained adventure is about. I hate to tell you, old friend, but I think she actually prefers me over you."

"That must be why she talks about you all the time."

"Truly?" Gibbs asked.

Tallon rolled his eyes. "Can we get on with this?" He could hear the edge in his voice. This was not a joking matter to him.

Scottie Barrett

He'd driven himself nearly mad wondering if Tess's obsession with Sloan had really tipped from hate to love. In Tallon's heart hid the hope that once Sloan was in prison, she would turn to him, that she would be able to concentrate on him, at least a little.

"You seem overly attached to the girl. It's not like you, Cliffe."

"She's the woman I intend to marry."

Gibbs, in his surprise, skidded on the edges of a greasy puddle. He groaned in disgust and shook the liquid off his boot. "Marry?"

A noise from behind made them both duck into a dark corner. They waited silently. A cat ran by with a freshly killed mouse.

They stepped out from their hiding place.

"I feel a right fool," Gibbs commented as he tucked the pistol back into his waistband. "How the devil did you get someone to say yes to you?"

"I'll worry about getting the yes later," Tallon said.

Gibbs stopped cold. "What makes you so sure there will be a yes?"

"There might not be a yes, but there will be a marriage."

"I guess I shouldn't be surprised. You never let her out of your sight. You poor devil," Gibbs said without sounding the least bit sympathetic.

Tallon led Gibbs down the alley behind Sloan's office. A woman standing in a recessed doorway lifted her dress to her waist and thrust her pelvis forward. Her voice thick with liquor, she made them an unintelligible offer. A man standing nearby took advantage and rubbed her with his filthy fingers.

"Why didn't you invite your ox-necked friend along? Two of

you big bastards stomping through this alley would have cleared it of any and all miscreants in a flash."

"Cyrus is busy watching over Tess. Here." Tallon handed Gibbs some coins and gestured in the couple's direction. "We need to get them inside. Go pay for his good time."

Unwilling to step too close, Gibbs threw the coins. They landed at the man's feet. "You two find a bed," Gibbs said with a grimace. "Hell, no man should have to witness *that*...ever," he mumbled to himself.

With gin-soaked laughter, the two disappeared into the building.

"Let's get in before anyone else comes," Tallon said.

Gibbs measured the width of the window with his hands. And then compared the distance with the breadth of Tallon's shoulders. "Never going to fit, old man."

"No, but you might."

"Oh, no! I'll get stuck and my legs will be dangling out in this criminal-infested alley."

Tallon laughed. "You don't actually think I planned on pushing that fat arse of yours through that small window? Just keep an eye out for me."

Tallon moved to stand in front of the alleyway door. While he worked the key into the lock, he hunched his back so it would appear as if he were taking a piss.

"How did you come by that key?"

"Jessup, naturally. He got a hold of Sloan's keys and made a copy."

"Well he truly is a marvel. I don't know why you would need me at all when Jessup is so capable."

Tallon shook his head. "I cannot believe you are still angry that he was promoted to captain before you." The lock released and Tallon, followed closely by Gibbs, pushed inside.

The furnishings consisted of a desk, a chair and a chest of drawers. Some hand-drawn maps were strewn across the desk. A lone painting hung forlornly on a moldy wall.

"It looks like he cleared this place out awhile ago," Gibbs said as he yanked open another empty drawer.

Tallon found nothing in the desk but a tin of tobacco and a crumpled handkerchief. Starting at the edges, Tallon paced the room, knocking the floorboards with the heel of his boot, listening for a hollow sound.

"There's not a damn thing here," Gibbs said.

Tallon, having discovered no cache in the floor, was in agreement. He strode to the window and with his sleeve swiped away a layer of grease. He peered out into the alley to see if it was safe to leave.

"I've found something," Gibbs said.

Tallon turned to see the gaping hole in the wall where the painting had been. Gibbs stuck in his hand and pulled out a cloth-wrapped bundle. "This is all there was," he said as he placed the package on the table, pulled the string and unfurled the flannel.

"Engraver's tools," Tallon remarked. But there were no incriminating etched plates.

"Not enough to get him arrested. Or to satisfy the soon-to-be Lady Marcliffe, I imagine," Gibbs said.

"Fucking hell," Tallon said with a biting laugh. He was a sorry bastard. He'd actually convinced himself that finding evidence which implicated Sloan would earn him Tess's affection.

Chapter Fifteen

Long before dawn, Tess found herself being ripped from her bed. She struggled in his arms against his impossibly hard chest. Flurry stood at the foot of the bed barking wildly, her protector looking like a tiny, white snowflake next to Lord Marcliffe.

A maid entered behind him carrying a traveling bag. After lighting a lamp, she started folding Tess's clothes and packing them in the valise.

Tess tried again to wriggle out of his grasp. He was as immovable as rock. "I'm not going anywhere with you."

"I say differently."

"You can't just order me about. I'm not one of your soldiers."

"Stop fighting me, or I'll carry you outside in your nightclothes."

As furious as she was, she knew she faced no danger. After all, he'd appointed Cyrus to be his eyes and ears, to make certain no harm came to her. "Fine. Set me down so I can at least get dressed."

With a heavy sigh, he dropped her none too gently to her feet. "You have two minutes."

"Yes, Captain Marcliffe," she said sulkily.

"I was a major, actually," he corrected and shut the door hard behind him.

To cover the angry marks Sloan had given her in the garden, she wrapped a fichu around her neck and tucked it into the neckline of her dress.

She could hear him pacing outside her door as she pinned up her hair. Her stomach felt queasy as she stepped into the hallway. Maybe this was the end of her London stay. Obviously, Lord Marcliffe had decided to dispense with his troublesome houseguest. She picked up Flurry and rubbed her face against his soft head. She would not be able to take care of a dog when she was cast out. It would be hard enough keeping herself fed.

With her night cap askew, Lady Stadwell stood in her doorway looking sleepy and befuddled. Tess ran to her. "Please take care of Flurry for me. He is very fond of you." She wrapped her arms around Lady Stadwell's frail shoulders, and the small dog let out a peep as he was caught amidst their embrace. "You are so dear to me."

Lady Stadwell patted her on the back. "Poor girl. Nephew, it is heartless of you not to be more forthright."

"In due time," Lord Marcliffe replied.

Tess let go of Lady Stadwell and clumsily swiped the wetness from her cheeks.

Lord Marcliffe picked up the valise, and Tess trailed obediently behind.

Craving the warmth and comfort of her bed, Tess stepped out into the chill dark of night. The coach and four awaited them. She had barely taken her seat across from Lord Marcliffe when the coach pulled abruptly away from the curb. To steady herself, she grabbed the overhead strap. The man was wasting no time ridding himself of her.

"If you'd provide me with enough fare to hire a carriage, you

176

could save yourself the trouble and drop me off right here." Brave words. She had no place to go. The tears threatened again.

"You're not getting away from me that easily." He sat back, crossing his arms over his chest, his muscles straining against the fabric of his sleeves.

Thinking of his big arms made her think of how he was big everywhere. It had been far too long since he had touched her intimately. To prevent herself from moaning, she pressed her knuckles to her lips. With effort, she pulled her gaze away.

She neatened her skirt then clutched her hands in her lap. "Fine then. Just keep all of this a mystery, and I will sit and hold my tongue."

He raised his eyebrow. "That would be a first."

She attempted unsuccessfully to concentrate on the bleakly shadowed scenery passing by the window. Her gaze was soon pulled back to Lord Marcliffe. A dark intensity radiated from him. He stretched out his legs, propping them on the bench beside her, effectively barring the exit, as though she might throw herself out of the hurtling coach.

They traveled hard and fast with Lord Marcliffe insisting on the breakneck pace as if someone were following them.

From the start of the baffling journey, he did not spend any time with her at the inns where they lodged. Instead, he saw to the changing of the horses. And in the evenings he haunted the local taverns. She would lie in the strange bed and cry herself to sleep wondering how she'd managed to make him hate her so much. And once ensconced in the coach again, he said not a word. When he wasn't sleeping, he was watching her as though she might evaporate before his eyes.

On the fourth day, she took her usual seat, and asked the same question she'd asked every single morning since they'd left London. "Where exactly are we going?"

He angled himself into the corner and sighed drowsily. "Do you remember my mentioning that Sloan had absconded to Scotland after his last crooked dealings?"

Shocked at getting a response, she sat forward. "No, I don't recall you telling me anything of the sort."

"Perhaps it was my aunt I spoke to. Now would you like me to continue?"

"Yes, although I hardly see what this has to do with you kidnapping me and dragging me across half the bloody country."

"Hell's fire, you are melodramatic, woman."

"Well, is it not true that I am your captive on this adventure?"

He leaned forward and took a firm grip of her wrist. He pushed her palm to his mouth and ran his tongue lightly across it. The erotic gesture instantly made her nipples hard.

"Believe me, sweeting, you would know if you were my captive." His tone was so sensual, she immediately felt heat swirling low in her belly.

"Please continue." Her voice cracked.

He gave her a carnal smile.

"I mean with your explanation," she clarified.

With reluctance, he released her wrist. His breathing had become heavier. He rubbed his face. "Now what the devil was I talking about?" he said more to himself than to her.

"Sloan and Scotland, remember?"

"Ah yes. My God, woman, my mind is always rattled when you are around. Anyhow, there is a man in Scotland who is said to be a master engraver. The kind of man who could create that near-perfect banknote. I think he is in league with Sloan."

178

"And why must I be here?"

"Isn't catching the bastard what motivates you? Shouldn't you be thanking me for asking you along?"

"How will my absence be explained to Sloan?"

"Cyrus will tell him you are ill. He can be quite convincing." He tipped his head back against the seat, his eyes drifting shut.

"Fortunately for you, you will not have to bear this dreadful journey twice in a month." She did not care that she sounded like a pouting child.

"Quiet, rabbit, I am trying to sleep."

ॐ

The driver slowed the coach to a crawl once they'd crossed into Scotland.

"Joseph Kerr," Lord Marcliffe said loudly, startling her from a stupor. "That is the man." He tapped on the roof of the coach. "Pull into that yard," he shouted.

Tess gazed out the window at the hostelry.

Lord Marcliffe pointed to a small placard in the yard. The name Joseph Kerr had been painted with enormous skill. Beneath the name was a picture of an anvil topped with a rose.

"He's an anvil priest, it seems, as well as a counterfeiter." He took the pistol from his waistband.

She put a restraining hand atop his. "What do you intend to do with that?"

His brow furrowed and he slid the pistol back into his waistband. "I suppose I could wait and see whether the man cooperates first."

"Please leave the pistol here," she pleaded.

"If you'd rather I didn't use the gun, then we'll have to go about it a different way." He glanced around the yard as if he were looking for inspiration. "I have it." He hid the pistol beneath the seat. "We'll obtain a certificate and bring it to the constable in London. He can then determine if the banknote is the work of the same man."

She agreed readily, thankful that she'd been able to dissuade him from intimidating the man with his pistol.

Her legs were wobbly as she stepped out of the coach. He secured her to his side as he led her up the path to a modest little house by the side of the inn.

"What type of document will you have him prepare?" she asked.

"A marriage certificate."

She stumbled. His arm tightened around her.

"A certificate produced by a master forger. You can't think it will have any validity. It will be a worthless piece of paper, nothing more," he assured her.

The door of the house burst open and a couple came springing out into the drizzly morning. They could not take their eyes from each other. *Is this what uncomplicated love looks like?* Tess wondered as they passed.

She grabbed at Lord Marcliffe's lapel. "We should tell them they are not really married."

He inclined his head in the direction of the house. A man garbed in a long black coat stood in the doorway. "Not a wise thing to do at this moment."

As they approached, the man offered them a generous, mostly toothless smile. "Joseph Kerr, at your service. A darling day for a wedding. It is a wedding you are after, right, sir?"

Lord Marcliffe nodded without hesitation.

The man ushered them into the small, dank home. With Lord Marcliffe's grip on her arm, Tess had no choice but to enter. A smoky haze hung over the room, making her eyes water.

Two older men with pipes clamped between their teeth got to their feet.

"I need a little fortification before I perform the next ceremony," Mr. Kerr said, and disappeared behind a partition of hanging blankets. The other men toddled after him.

She balked, refusing to move farther into the interior. "He is dressed like a cleric."

"He also reeks of drink, and clearly he's gone off to get more. It is a costume. He is playing at being a preacher." His fingers wrapped tighter around her arm and propelled her forward. "Just think, the next time you come to Gretna Green you will be quite familiar with the proceedings. Not near so nervous." His gaze fixed on her trembling lips.

The trio pushed through the gap in the blankets and Mr. Kerr took a seat at a makeshift desk fashioned from an ancient door.

Lord Marcliffe placed a packet atop the scarred wood surface. The man tipped the packet, spilling out the gold coins. It looked to be a hundred guineas or more. It struck Tess that Mr. Kerr was not used to such a generous payment. He tested one coin between his teeth, ironically trying to see if it was counterfeit, before slowly and methodically stacking the coins.

"Mr. Kerr, I'd appreciate it if you'd get on with this." Lord Marcliffe tossed a few more coins atop the pile as an incentive. "My betrothed is getting a little anxious."

The man dipped his pen and held the quill poised above the certificate. "Your name, sir?"

"Tallon Michael Hawkes, the Earl of Marcliffe and Viscount

Bromley."

She was shocked to find he'd provided the man with his real name.

"And yours, lass?"

"Horten—"

"Tess Starling," Lord Marcliffe spoke over her. His breath was warm against her ear. "Don't fret so. You will make him suspicious."

"'Tis your own free will that brings you here, lass?" Mr. Kerr asked.

The whole thing seemed too real. She scrutinized Lord Marcliffe's face for signs of deceit. He appeared as innocent as a dark angel. No different, actually, from how he always looked.

"Pardon us for a moment," he said, and pulled her aside. "Haven't you heard that Gretna Green marriages are always performed by a blacksmith?"

She could vaguely recall hearing something like that.

"Mr. Kerr, what is your primary occupation?" she asked.

The old man looked up from his treasure. He'd begun counting his coins again. "I'm a saddler, Miss Starling."

Lord Marcliffe winked at her. "Forger, saddler, anvil priest. The man's a jack-of-all-trades," he whispered in her ear.

She remained unconvinced. His answers were too glib. But her naiveté about elopements put her at a disadvantage. If a man was desperate to bed a woman, but averse to marrying her, wouldn't a sham preacher be just the thing? When the rakehell's lust was slaked, he could simply dispose of the certificate, and it would be his word against hers.

Perhaps she was being too cynical. She glanced at Mr. Kerr. Sot or not, there was something sincere in his bloodshot eyes. Lord Marcliffe made a show of removing his pocket watch from his waistcoat and glanced from it to Tess. Still balancing the watch on his palm, he shook his head indulgently. It was certainly a grand performance he was putting on for Mr. Kerr's benefit.

She shot him an annoyed look. She was not done thinking yet. It would behoove her to ask the most relevant question. It was at the tip of her brain, but she could not bring herself to voice it. It would be supreme conceit to think the earl had actually gone to such lengths to wed her. To ascribe such romantic motives to a man who bent her to her knees to fulfill his desires was beyond absurd. She turned back to Mr. Kerr. "I am here of my own free will," she said with a sigh.

Lord Marcliffe put the quill to paper then handed it to her. "It won't hurt to sign it. It is, after all, a worthless document," he said, his lips so close they grazed her ear.

By now Mr. Kerr was beginning to look a bit uneasy with all the whispering. Tess was worried he would figure out why they were really there, so she complied.

Her signature looked frail beside Lord Marcliffe's bold scrawl. The certificate was impressive. Mr. Kerr had filled out their information in a beautiful calligraphic hand.

"Put the pipes out, boys." Mr. Kerr motioned to the old men smoking in the corner.

Mr. Kerr began to recite the marriage ceremony from a battered book. Lord Marcliffe was right, he looked anything but a man of God. On closer inspection, she noticed the patches and oily stains on his coat. Though Tess stood more than an arm's reach from the man, the alcohol on his breath assaulted her nose.

For no reason she could gather, the faux ceremony made her nervous. Watching Mr. Kerr with his facial tics did not help. After finding that a corner of her lip was twitching in unconscious imitation, she turned her head and peered up at Lord Marcliffe. He looked far too relaxed to her way of thinking. What an unhappy day, she thought, to be pretending to marry the person you loved. With a gentle squeeze of her hand, he prodded her to repeat her lines.

She recited her vows as though listing ingredients from a recipe.

"Have you a ring?" Mr. Kerr asked.

Lord Marcliffe removed a heavy ring from his finger. It was inscribed with a coat of arms. She had never seen him wear it before. "I hope this will do," he said to her.

"You are oddly prepared for this." Doubt of his motives continued to plague her.

To keep the huge ring from sliding off her finger, she folded her hand into a fist.

At the end of the ceremony, the three old men stared at Lord Marcliffe and Tess as if waiting for something. Mr. Kerr mumbled something under his breath.

"What was that?" Lord Marcliffe asked.

"The kiss, man, the kiss."

Tess froze, and it seemed her partner had gone just as rigid. They had clearly not thought out the entire ruse. He leaned over and gave her a quick peck on the cheek. The expression on Mr. Kerr's face crumpled with disappointment. The witnesses shook their heads. Lydia Midwinter had been right. He had no inclination for kissing.

Tess pushed his guiding hand away as they walked back to the carriage. Endless days on the road and all they had to show for it was a fake certificate. She did not even get a proper kiss for all her troubles.

"What a ridiculous charade," she complained as she

climbed into the coach. "I hope that was worth it."

"It was," Lord Marcliffe said, and patted the document in his pocket.

"You are so sure of yourself. What if you have the wrong forger?"

He smiled. "No, he was the right man. I'm certain of it."

She looked wistfully at the ring still enfolded in her hand. With reluctance, she handed it to him.

"You keep it safe for me."

Bloody wonderful. No kiss, but now she had a souvenir to remind her of the wedding that would never be. She wrapped it in a linen handkerchief and placed it in her reticule.

&

The sun was still high in the sky when Tess woke from her nap and found herself alone in the carriage. She rubbed the kink out of her neck. They were stopped in front of a small inn, its stone exterior covered with moss. She found Lord Marcliffe inside making room arrangements.

"We are through traveling for the day?" she asked him. "There is still so much daylight."

"I've grown weary of the road," he said.

A servant picked up their bags and led them upstairs. The boy pushed open the door of the first room they came to, and Tess entered. Lord Marcliffe followed her into the chamber.

"If you prefer this room, Lord Marcliffe, I have no problem taking another."

He dismissed the boy then pushed the door shut with his foot and stared at her. The situation seemed suddenly awkward. "You do realize that even these small inns have their gossip channels to town." Though it was a little late to worry about her reputation, seeing how she had just traveled nearly the length of England unchaperoned.

He grabbed her to him. "Let them talk. What could be interesting about a man spending the night at an inn with his wife?"

"Very amusing." She tried to push out of his iron clasp.

He crushed her tighter to him. "There is nothing amusing about it, Tess. We are married."

She wriggled angrily out of his arms. "You are not making the least sense."

He leaned back against the door and folded his arms across his chest. His eyes hooded, he studied her through his long black lashes. "I think I'm being quite clear. We're married, Tess, simple as that. The ceremony was no hoax."

"But that man was a forger."

"I lied. I saw the fancy script Mr. Kerr used to advertise his business. I thought perhaps he'd show the same skill filling out the marriage form, and, thankfully, he did."

"Why?" was the only word she could muster, her voice sounding thin and reedy.

"Because you would have gone through with it—you would have married Sloan. I needed to protect you from yourself. I tried again and again to warn you, you have no idea how dangerous a man like Sloan is."

Of course she knew how deadly Sloan was. His threat against Lord Marcliffe was chillingly clear in her mind. Tess would never allow Sloan to destroy another man she loved. She'd kept her neck swathed in fabric the entire trip, hiding her secret beneath fichus and shawls or high-collared jackets.

Today she was wearing a Spencer over a scoop-necked muslin, the only thing she'd had left in her valise that was presentable. With reluctance, she removed her jacket. "I know very well how dangerous a man he can be." She whipped off the fichu. "And I find it rather exhilarating."

"Christ." His eyes narrowed to furious slits. "So you prefer sexual intercourse to be a little more *punishing*." His fingers pressed not so tenderly on the three fading spots circling her neck like a hideous necklace. "Marking his property, was he?" he sneered. "And you, aren't you the cunning one?"

"We could rip up that license, and no one would be the wiser." Her heart was breaking, to give up the man she cherished.

"Burn it for all I care." He took the license from his pocket and flung it at her. "Thank you for a memorable wedding night," he said, his gaze shifting away as though he couldn't bear to look at her.

He stalked to the window and threw it open. "Hold the carriage, man," he shouted down to the courtyard. He strode past Tess. "I'm leaving. If you want a ride back to London, you'd best hurry."

The moment the door shut behind him, she muffled her sobs with her fichu. She cursed her revenge-fueled obsession with Sloan. It had been the cause of so much pain. With care, Tess picked up the parchment and folded it before slipping it into her reticule. The glint of the ring inside caught her attention. She pulled it out and placed it on her finger. She felt an ache in her chest. For reasons she could not explain, she plucked out a hair ribbon from her reticule and slid the ring onto it. The yellow satin tickled the skin on her neck as she tied it hastily and dropped the heavy ring down her chemise.

Chapter Sixteen

A sprinkling of raindrops dampened her hair as Tess walked to the coach. Once seated, she made herself small in the corner opposite from Lord Marcliffe. Without sparing her a glance, he rapped the ceiling and the horses were off. How would she survive this torturous trip home? She congratulated herself for being a terrifically intuitive spy. In Gretna Green, she'd fretted that there was trickery afoot. But her suspicions had too conveniently reflected her own romantic yearnings so she'd given them short shrift. And the man who'd put to rest her qualms had been far too convincing. Now he was her husband.

The world outside darkened into a somber shade. Soon rain slashed against the windows. Even with the rainfall and solid ceiling of clouds above, Tess thought it would still be less gloomy sitting alongside the driver on the box than being locked inside with Lord Marcliffe's black mood.

Tess believed it was only concern for the horses that finally made Lord Marcliffe order the carriage to a stop. Otherwise, she was certain he would have risked traveling blind in the pitch-black night if it would get him to London faster. *And away from her.*

The next morning, after exiting another stone cottage more moss-covered than the last, Tess braced herself for another day closeted with a man who wished her to hell.

He looked away as she climbed aboard the coach. His jaw was set and his fingers, curled into loose fists, rested on his spread thighs. Chilling anger seemed to radiate from him. Thankfully, she'd thought to wind a scarf around her neck. In his temper, there was no point in reminding him of the bruises.

The road had been beaten by the night's heavy rain and every hole and rock had been exposed. The driver seemed to be taking malicious pleasure in hitting every single one of them. The carriage took a dip at reckless speed, and Tess banged her head against the edge of the window. The driver seemed to be feeding off Lord Marcliffe's to-the-devil attitude.

The carriage lurched again. Before Tess could stop herself, she smacked the door handle hard with her elbow. Her eyes watering, she sat back and rubbed her sore arm. Miffed, she noticed Lord Marcliffe, still sitting like a bronze cast statue, completely undeterred by the violent rocking. Just as the tingling subsided in her arm, the driver hit another hole head on, and she flew off the seat and found herself sprawled over Lord Marcliffe's legs. His heavy hand gave her a sharp tap on the bottom.

"Don't tempt me, woman."

She scrambled off his lap and wedged herself back into the corner, determined to stay put. She stared out the window and the bleak scenery kept repeating. Suddenly, it felt as if the interior of the carriage was shrinking. Convinced that there was a shortage of air, she put her gloved hands to her mouth and tried to yawn deeply. It felt as if she were not getting enough breath. Her lips tingled, and she was sure she would swoon.

"Why are you fidgeting so?"

She fanned herself. "There's not enough air in here."

He gave her a confounded look.

Tess started to hum to herself trying hard not to think about breathing. Abruptly, she stopped her humming and pressed her cheek against the moist cold pane. "I need conversation. I'm going mad inside this box."

"Let's see if I can find an interesting subject," he drawled. He rubbed his stubbled chin. "Ah, here's a slice of information that might occupy your mind. Destroying that license did not erase the marriage. If you'll recall, we had an audience. Joseph Kerr and his friends authenticated the ceremony."

Tess straightened. "Certainly it cannot be that difficult to void an unconsummated marriage."

"No court would believe it unless it could be proved that I was impotent. And that, sweeting, can be disproved by a number of witnesses."

"How terribly charming." All of her maladies seemed to have disappeared because now she was too busy being angry. "Enough conversation."

He stacked his hands behind his head and closed his eyes, obviously well pleased with himself.

At the next inn she insisted on a bath. Knowing that this would be the highlight of the horrendous trip, she relished every moment in the water. Unfortunately, the water pouring down from the sky did nothing to lighten her spirits. She stepped out of the inn clean and shiny and trudged through the mud to the coach.

By midday, they reached yet another obscure little village.

The wheels squished through the mud as the coach rolled to a stop. Instantly, Lord Marcliffe was up and out the door. "Stay with the horses," he called up to the driver, "I'll bring you a pint."

The humidity in the carriage made Tess feel like she was being smothered in wet wool. She found herself counting the breaths she was taking in, fretting about the lack of air again. She flew out the door and ran toward the tavern, not heeding the driver's pleas to return.

The smoke-filled air inside was not much of an improvement, but at least she was no longer trapped in the traveling tomb. If she could locate Lord Marcliffe through the haze, he could spare her a sip or more of spirits to calm her nerves. There were certainly spirits to be found here. The smell of alcohol seemed to pour from the damp walls. And the patrons had done more than calm themselves. Many drowsed on benches. There were a few men slumped in corners. Tess stepped carefully over the ale puddled on the rotting floorboards.

It suddenly occurred to her that her presence was causing a bit of a stir. Two men lounging on a bench by the hearth sat up suddenly. One of the men thumped the other in the chest as she passed. The tavern maid gave her a wink as Tess sidled around a table in the center of the room. With relief, she spotted him. His back was to her, his head in his hand, a tankard at his elbow.

Fingers clamped on to her arm and she startled. One of the men from the hearth had followed her. "Pretty strangers don't walk in here often."

She cringed at the stale odor of ale on his breath. "Please get your hand off of me!"

At the sound of her voice, Lord Marcliffe whipped around with such force that the bench upturned. Instantly he had the man by the throat. The crowd parted.

"Wife, get out of here," he said in a voice that sent a shiver up her spine.

She shoved her way through the onlookers. Once in the yard, she began pacing. The mud seeped through her satin slippers and dragged down her hem. The rain beaded on her lashes and made her ringlets droop. How fearsome Lord Marcliffe could be. She sincerely hoped he was not pulling off the man's head. His offense had not been that great. Suddenly, it was all too humorous. She was protecting Lord Marcliffe, a man who needed no protection.

Soon he was stomping across the yard, his long black coat flying behind him. He grabbed her wrist and yanked her along.

Her heart raced at the thought of climbing back in the coach. His fury would most definitely suck up all the air inside. She planted her heels firmly into the wet ground. Her hands and face were tingling and her head spun.

"Just leave me here. I will fend for myself."

"It is only one more day. You've gone this far," he said.

She tried to wrench free from his grip. "Please, I cannot bear to go in there with your being the way you are." He released her and she ran away from the tavern, across the road to a stand of trees. She leaned back against a tree and shut her eyes. When she opened them he was staring down at her.

"How do you mean, 'the way I am'?"

"You're miserable. And I hate that you hate me, when I was only trying to keep you safe. Don't you see, the entire thing about Sloan—it's not about revenge anymore." She unwound the scarf from her neck. "What I witnessed in the tavern made me realize my folly. In my entire life I have never known a more formidable man." She pressed her fingers to the bruises on her bared throat. "These marks came with a threat. Marry him or *Marcliffe dies.*"

"Well, I will have to kill the bastard."

192

"No. No. You must promise not to go near him," she pleaded.

He reached forward and caressed the marks. His fingers found the ribbon, and she felt the ring sliding up her cleavage. His dimple made a startling appearance. A lump formed in her throat. It had been so long since she'd seen that smile.

His gaze focused on the ring.

She wiggled her ring finger. "I suppose I will need to plump up a bit for it to fit."

"You are already plump in all the right places." Wrapping the cord around his hand, he reeled her forward. His other hand snaked around her waist. She toppled into his arms. He enveloped her in his warmth as his open mouth slammed over hers.

His tongue invaded her mouth, rubbing against hers with possessive roughness. She gripped his shoulders and pressed her shivering body into his heat. When he lifted his head, she felt dizzy.

He dipped his head again, stroking his tongue over the seam of her lips. She responded by opening her mouth to his delicious tongue. She sucked it hard, eliciting a primal groan from deep in his throat.

Breathless with surprise, she pulled away. "For a man who doesn't like kissing—"

"Do shut up, rabbit," he said and slanted his mouth over hers again. Both hands slid over her hips to firmly cup her bottom.

There were angry shouts in the distance, and he lifted his head. "Damn it." He glanced over his shoulder at the tavern. "It might be better if we vacate this village. Do you think you can get into the carriage now?"

She grabbed his thick forearm. "You didn't kill the man, did you?"

He took hold of the hand that gripped his sleeve. "What kind of a monster do you take me for? Let's just say he was a bit shaken. I see the driver has anticipated me."

The horses stopped a few feet from them. The crowd at the tavern seemed to settle down. They stared and pointed at the coat of arms on the side. "No doubt, you will be their topic of conversation for the next few days," Tess said.

Tess felt quite at ease as she entered the coach.

"Make haste," Lord Marcliffe ordered the driver as he climbed in after her. There was the sound of a whip cracking the air then the vehicle lurched forward.

The carriage was no longer oppressive, but cozy. Apparently, it had been his mood that had made her so anxious.

Up till now, Lord Marcliffe had seated himself as far away from her as possible. She had done the same. But now she was nearly in his lap. He began removing her rain-soaked Spencer. "Lord Marcliffe, what are you doing?"

"My aunt would never forgive me if I brought you home ill. It is obvious that these wet garments must be removed for the sake of your health."

He pushed the jacket off her shoulders and leaned in to kiss her throat. The wet muslin of the dress clung to her body as he slid it from her shoulders, chemise and all. His cool, wet kisses trailed down the white skin of her breasts, and she pushed against his lips. "Of course," she said in a breathless whisper, "we should wait to consummate this marriage until after we arrive—" His teeth lightly pulled on her erect nipple and she gasped. "—home." Her fingers tangled in his hair, and she held his head as his mouth made every inch of her skin shiver. "It would be the proper thing to do." Her words were barely audible.

He lifted his face and kissed her ear. "Indeed," he whispered as his fingers inched the dress lower, leaving her naked to the waist. The thin fabric, made even more vulnerable with moisture, nearly ripped as he slid her clothing off her hips and out from under her. He lit the interior lantern and stared at her hungrily as he plunked down hard on the seat across from her and undid his trousers.

"Part your legs."

The instant she obeyed and spread her thighs, he slid his finger into her and simultaneously swept his tongue over her nipple. Her hand glided through his smooth, black hair. His finger explored her, and she felt moisture between her thighs. He hooked his finger through the ring that dangled between her breasts and tugged her closer, so that the stiff peak of her nipple found its way to his mouth. His mouth moved to her other breast. He pulled the nipple through his teeth and sucked hard.

He raised his head. "My wife," he said as he dropped the ring so that it dangled once again between her breasts.

Both his hands worked her quim now. While one was continually stroking the downy hair or parting her nether lips and rubbing the exposed inner folds, the other was thrusting into her with a driving rhythm. It gave her a thrill to look down on his dark head and see that he watched everything he was doing to her. Her legs felt like jelly, and she dug her fingers into the hard muscles of his shoulders.

He pressed his face into her belly. "I need to have you, Tess," he said, his voice raw.

After maneuvering her, he positioned himself on his knees between her splayed legs. He spread her nether lips with one

Scottie Barrett

hand and rubbed the thumb of his other hand over the tender slick folds then swirled it deliciously over her nub. Tess shuddered with ecstasy. Moving forward, he guided his shaft. She could feel it prodding where his finger had been moments before.

Still on his knees, he gripped her bottom, angling her toward him.

"Tess." He nearly growled her name as he forced an entry into her narrow passage. She inhaled a startled breath. He was so thick, she felt as if she were being stretched to the extreme.

"Do you want more of me?" he asked. He pushed in another spine-tingling notch.

"I want all of you," she said, her voice cracking.

His fingers dug into her bottom, holding her firm. He rammed into her in one solid stroke. Tess gripped his shoulders, stunned for a second, impaled on his massive cock. The coach dipped hard. "Tallon," she cried. It felt like a delicious punishment. She squirmed, exalting in the unbelievable feel of him being inside her.

He groaned. "Tess, stop moving," he said through gritted teeth, as though he were about to lose control. He reached around the small of her back and pulled her hips toward him. Her legs wrapped around his waist, holding tightly to him. His mouth slanted over hers, his tongue plunging deep to tangle with hers. His hips lifted, dragging his rigid shaft out of her then he drove into her again. His tongue simulated the same hard-riding rhythm of his cock. Reaching between them, his callused fingers found her most sensitive spot. He caressed her nub with exquisite skill. Her body reacted instantly, her tight sheathe spasming around him. He clutched her hips, pressing his fingers into her naked skin, and shoved deeply into her one more time, bringing his body to a shuddering climax.

A soft moan escaped her lips as he slid his cock out. He rose off his knees, sat back on the seat. He stared at the telltale pink stain on the hem of his shirt and grinned before pulling her into his lap.

His fingers trailed deliciously up and down her back. "You would have made a delectable mistress. But I much prefer you as my wife." Reaching up, he twined one of her curls around his finger. "It's extraordinary how the color changes with every degree of light."

Tess drew her thumb over his sensuous bottom lip. "Lydia lied. She said you never kissed your mistress."

"She didn't lie. That was a business relationship." He took a coil of her hair and brushed the ends across her nipple.

"And our relationship—"

"Is based on passion." He grabbed a handful of her hair and inhaled.

"I wish you to end your *business* relationship." She was already overstepping her bounds as his wife. Men in his position often kept a mistress. Yet, she found it impossible to prevent her lips from pushing into a pout.

"And if I choose to continue it?" He stopped stroking her for a moment. He seemed intent on her answer.

"I would leave you," she said simply. Her eyes filled with tears. She refused to share him. One kiss and she wanted to have him completely.

His gaze grew tender. "I haven't paid a visit to the woman since I've met you. It has long been over."

"It was Hortensia you met in the beginning," she reminded him. Merely thinking of her drab incarnation made her wince.

"That is exactly when I ended the affair—when I first met Hortensia. And I must say, sometimes I wish for her back, although without the fake eyebrows...and the ratty wig." He tugged gently at her nipple.

She reached past him and plucked her clothes from the seat. As her dress swept by him he seized it. It was a bit of a struggle to wrest it from his grasp. Finally, after heaving a frustrated sigh, he cooperated and helped her wriggle into her still damp clothes. Tucked blissfully in his arms, she snuggled against his chest.

Chapter Seventeen

They passed through Grosvenor Square and Tess could hardly contain herself. The townhouse was minutes away. A heavy fog made visibility poor. As the third stories of the row of houses loomed above the gray mist, Tess pressed her face to the window. The brick façade was shrouded, but the glow of a cigar butt could be seen in front of the house. "Cyrus!" she exclaimed and laughed aloud.

"What is so amusing?" Tallon peered out the window.

"Nothing really. It's just that I'm so excited to be getting out of this carriage."

"I don't know, I thought this last day of travel was rather enjoyable." His gaze traveled from her lips to her feet. "Although I would have preferred you to stay completely naked for the duration."

Tess was not entirely certain that her wobbly legs would support her once she stepped onto solid ground.

As huge as Cyrus was he nearly vanished in the thick cloud of moisture swirling around him. He waved some of the floating particles away from his face and squinted toward the carriage before hurrying inside.

"I'm sure my aunt has not left yet. She had planned to ship off to her country house for the warm months." The horses stopped and, not waiting for the driver, Tallon threw open the door, stepped out and turned to give Tess his hand. "Lady Marcliffe." The flirtatious smile he offered her as she accepted his hand made her heart race. Overnight her life had changed. She'd gone from pure misery to complete ecstasy. If she was dreaming, may she never wake up.

Cyrus returned outside with Lady Stadwell, Flurry at her heels barking wildly.

"Nephew, you shocked me," Lady Stadwell called. "I did not expect you so soon. As you see, I have not vacated the townhouse as of yet. But I will make haste and leave sooner."

Tess rushed up the steps. "It is good to see you, Lady Stadwell."

"Now, now, what is with all the formalities? I insist you call me Aunt." She grinned widely as she took Tess's hands. "Since we are related."

"You knew what he was up to then?" Suddenly Lady Stadwell's demeanor and words on the night Tallon had abducted her made sense.

Lady Stadwell placed the soft palm of her hand against Tess's cheek. "Of course, my dear, and I couldn't be happier. Now come inside for some tea. You must be weary."

Tess ran upstairs to change out of her wrinkled clothes. Flurry, still yapping a greeting, followed her. She took her time getting ready. Tess needed to absorb the earth-shattering events of the last day.

At the washstand, she freshened up with the lavender soap then tamed her curls with her silver-backed brush. She plucked the necklace from the mirror frame and fastened it around her neck. The diamonds sparkled wickedly at her. The extravagant gift reminded her of their provocative history. No words of love had been spoken. Was she his wife or a mistress with a marriage certificate?

Tess strolled back down to the parlor.

"The tea is nearly cold, my dear," Lady Stadwell said. "She's here now. I do wish you would take a seat, Nephew."

But he didn't. Instead, he walked circles around the room, putting Tess in mind of a sleek panther pacing. He seemed anxious to get the tea party over with.

Tess spoke of their travels and the marriage ceremony in the lightest of tones, smoothing over the rough patches of their trip so as not to worry Lady Stadwell. Though she did not appear to be completely convinced of the uncomplicated story Tess told, she listened attentively.

"Did Mr. Sloan come by?" Tess kept her voice flat and did not look at her husband when she asked the question.

Lady Stadwell lifted her gaze heavenward. "Have you seen the calling cards in the platter in the hallway? The devil came every day. The servants were instructed to say you were ill. That is until Cyrus told him the truth. Once we'd determined there wasn't a chance Sloan could catch your coach, Cyrus informed him of the elopement." She wiped her hands as though she'd just dispensed with rubbish. "We never heard from Sloan again."

Tess did not express her doubts, but she did not believe that villainous characters disappeared so conveniently from one's life.

With a wry smile, Lady Stadwell eyed her nephew's restlessness and declared, "A newlywed couple needs some time alone, and I'm determined to leave at once."

And true to her word, with very little fuss she departed at noon with a few of Tallon's serving staff.

∞

That night, Tess chose a lace-edged nightrail. It was a clinging silk piece meant only for seduction, based on a design suggested by her courtesan tutor. Tess entered the bedchamber from the dressing room to find her husband sitting in a chair working his boots off. He was fully clothed as she'd expected.

"Finally," he said. "How long does it take to put on a scrap of material?" His gaze followed her as she climbed into bed beneath the covers.

"I wanted to look my best. It is officially my first night with my husband. The carriage doesn't count." In truth, her husband's pacing outside her door had flustered her.

"It counts," he contradicted.

"Well, maybe it counts a little." She arranged her just-brushed hair over her shoulders.

He dropped his boots beside the chair. "Snuff the candle."

She turned on her side and propped herself on her elbow. "Let's leave it burning."

With a bemused look, he got to his feet and removed his coat, cravat and waistcoat. Tess knew exactly what was to follow. After depositing his garments on the chair, he stepped toward the bed stand with the clear intent of putting out the light, just as she'd predicted. She swung out of bed and snatched up the candle. "If you do not shed all your clothes tonight then I shall sleep in a flannel gown buttoned to the neck and a robe."

"Did you think I would sleep with my trousers on?"

"Oh, stubborn man, let me see them."

He waggled his brows and offered a suggestive smile complete with dimple.

She gave an exasperated sigh. "You know exactly what I

mean."

He pressed his hand to his shoulder. "What, so I can scare you off when I've only just talked you into my bed?"

"Then a flannel gown it shall be." Candle still in hand, she started toward the dressing room.

"Frightening. That was your word for them, if you recall." He tugged off his shirt and practically dared her to look at him. But she kept her focus on his eyes until he'd shed his trousers and drawers. Then she allowed her gaze to roam over his intimidating physique.

She set down the candle and approached him. "I said they were fascinating as well." She stroked her fingertips gently over the scar on his shoulder. The wounds had been great. If things had gone differently, she very well might never have known him. She pressed a kiss to the seamed skin. His body gave a jolt beneath her hands.

"I have another one," he said. Instantly, it seemed, he'd forgotten his worries and relished the attention.

"I had no intention of neglecting it." She smiled up at him. Her hands smoothed down the length of his muscular body as she lowered herself to her knees, her tongue tracing a trail down his chest to his rock-hard abdomen then along his hipbone. Purposefully, she detoured a bit and brushed her cheek against his throbbing cock before licking her way down to his thigh. She lavished his other scar with open-mouthed kisses.

"Now I want my cock in your sweet mouth." He put his fingers under her chin and lifted her gently. Her mouth opened greedily on him. She swirled her tongue around his shaft.

"On the bed," he ordered almost instantly.

With a pout on her lips, Tess sat back on her heels. He tasted delicious and she wanted more of him. Apparently, her husband was in an indecisive mood. It seemed he wished her everywhere at once. Acceding to his newest demand, she stretched herself out on the bed.

He pointed to the nightrail. "Off," he said simply.

She sat up and pulled the shimmering gown over her head and let it slither from her fingers to puddle on the floor.

"So, Tess," Tallon said as he settled himself between her legs. He slid her hair aside to bare her breasts. "How do you enjoy being Lady Marcliffe?" The last words he whispered, and her body answered with a tremble.

"It is a tolerable situation thus far." She accommodated his big body by splaying her knees farther apart. She smoothed her hands over his back.

"Tolerable, you say?" He lifted himself and entered her slowly. "Would you say—" he pushed into her in exquisite increments, "—barely tolerable or—" his cock seemed to reach the deepest part of her "—or quite tolerable?"

Breathless, she clung to him. He rode her with a possessive rhythm that sent her senses reeling.

"Tess!" he cried as he collapsed atop her, spilling his seed inside her.

As they settled into sleep, his body curled tightly against her back, she finally managed to answer his question. "Quite tolerable," she said.

༄

Tallon woke to the smell of burning bread and, finding the bed empty, assumed Tess was downstairs making breakfast. He congratulated himself for disconcerting her so thoroughly that she'd botched her baking.

In a hurry to tease his new bride about her mishap in the kitchen, Tallon beckoned Cyrus with the bell pull.

With his usual lack of grace, Tallon's new valet barreled into the room. Without being asked, Cyrus began sharpening the razor on the strop. "I do wish that infernal bell would break. Couldn't you shout for me, sir?"

"Just not done, old man." Tallon soaped his face. "What's burning?"

"A pan of buns." Cyrus clicked his tongue. "A shame. They looked tasty. We have Jane to blame for that. That pesky wench took Lady Marcliffe out into the garden with some nonsense about the dog digging up the flowers. How that little pup could do any damage, I don't know."

Tallon turned to him, his face half lathered.

"Something's not right with that wench. Always seemed to be lurking about when I was telling Mr. Sloan to bugger off," Cyrus continued.

A chilling dread knocked the breath out of Tallon. The pieces had fallen into order for him. He'd made certain not to pick Jane to help Tess pack for the elopement. But he had only suspected the maid of being a gossip. It had never occurred to him that there was anything more sinister about her. He grabbed the towel from Cyrus's shoulder and wiped his face. He pulled on his shirt and raced down the stairs. Cyrus's loud steps thundered behind him.

Jane looked up from the washboard as Tallon burst into the kitchen. Her face turning ashen, she dropped the wet clothing into the tub and curtsied low. "My lord."

"Where's Lady Marcliffe?"

"I have yet to see her this morning."

Cyrus skidded in behind Tallon. "You lying wench, I saw

you with her not more than thirty minutes ago when you were dragging her into the garden."

Tallon narrowed the distance between himself and the maid. "Where is she?"

Jane blinked rapidly and retreated a step.

With the flat of his hand, Tallon slammed the wall above her head.

Jane flinched. "At Mr. Sloan's cottage in Woolwich. Unless the boat's sailed."

"I'll fetch your horse." Cyrus was already clumping up the basement stairs.

"You follow with the coach for Lady Marcliffe. I'll need some way to bring my wife home," Tallon called up to him.

Tess would be coming home because for Tallon, there was no other possibility.

Chapter Eighteen

Sloan uncorked the bottle and poured a glass of green liquid.

"Poison?" Tess asked almost politely before Sloan leaned across the table, pinched her chin hard and forced her jaw open. He shoved pills into her mouth then thrust the glass of the green liquid into her hands. It was quite awkward to drink with her wrists bound together with rope, but she gulped the liquid the best she could, chasing down the bitter pills with the bitter drink. A trickle ran down her chin. She lifted her shoulder and wiped it off on her dress.

Tess surveyed her surroundings again. From its ordinary exterior no one would guess how the cottage was furnished. The settee was upholstered in gold damask, as was the ottoman. The small dining table was elaborately carved with gilded dragons twining up the legs. The table chairs had cushions with golden tassels. She looked back at her captor with his pomaded curls and decided the tasteless setting fit him perfectly.

"I'm glad you are no longer trying to vomit. Frightfully expensive stuff." Sloan studied her. "That, my dear, is a devastating mix—Spanish fly and wormwood liquor. I'm surprised you haven't felt the effects yet. You've had enough to stimulate a horse."

"I suppose this is the only way you can get women to share your bed."

"Actually, most are quite willing. But for a betraying bitch like yourself, it isn't enough that you be willing. I want you to come crawling to me. I want to hear you beg."

In truth, Tess had been feeling the effects of the aphrodisiacs for quite some time. She shifted uncomfortably in her chair. Her quim was soaking wet and aching to be touched. But, even under the influence of his potions, she didn't want the bastard touching her. That was about the only thing she could still reason out. Her thoughts were almost entirely controlled by the sensations concentrated in her quim. Even the gun he waved was merely a glinting distraction that her eyes followed as a child might a shiny toy. Nothing seemed real.

"I want you obedient when you travel with me to China. Not as my bride, of course, but as an offering. A whore with your exotic coloring would be quite a novelty. Anyone who can be of service to me will be offered a suck or a fuck. And for those willing to pay, I will let them use you for any perverted tendency they may wish to indulge."

The door of the cottage burst open. It was obvious by the look in his eyes that Tallon had heard the last of Sloan's speech. Though he brandished a pistol, he looked like he'd relish tearing out the man's throat with his bare hands.

Sloan jumped to his feet, swung his arm to the right and took aim at Tess's head. "Must have ridden here hell-bent for leather. I'd hoped to have her naked before you arrived. Predictable Jane. Foolish baggage, did exactly as I'd expected." Through the slight quivering of the gun, Tess could see that Sloan's hand trembled. The fear was justified. The rage seemed to vibrate off Tallon, yet the solid set of his jaw and the steely gaze gave him an aura of menacing calm. He looked like an emissary from hell. "Now put the pistol here where I can see it."

With cautious movements, Tallon approached and set his gun on the table.

Sloan kicked his chair aside and shifted closer to Tess. "I know your nature, man. You've come equipped with more arms than that. Get rid of them all, Marcliffe."

From his waistcoat pocket Tallon withdrew a palm-sized gun and placed it beside the pistol.

"Let's see what you've got tucked in your boots."

He pulled a small dagger from the top of each of his Hessians. Those, too, joined the deadly little pile. After removing his coat, he turned in a circle to show that he'd relinquished all his weapons.

Tess watched her husband from beneath lazy, hooded lids. Their eyes met.

"What have you given her?"

Sloan shrugged. "Handfuls of a potent aphrodisiac I purchased from an unscrupulous apothecary. I believe she is aching for a man's attention right about now. Isn't that right, Tess?"

Tess gave Tallon a smile that was raw with sexuality. He blinked at her in confusion. From the moment he'd burst into the room, his black hair wild around his face, she'd felt an immediate need for him. She would have thrown herself at him if she hadn't had her wrists bound.

At the sound of metal scraping on wood, Tess turned. The pistol Sloan aimed at her wavered as he used his free hand to sweep Marcliffe's weaponry toward him. He began lining the daggers and guns up side by side. "Why ever did you marry Marcliffe? He's such a barbaric son of a bitch."

"I didn't choose to. He tricked me." She winced as she said

the words. The intoxicants had loosened her tongue. And the sight of her dizzyingly handsome husband had not helped the matter. "But look at him. He's everything a woman could want." She shivered with lust. *"He's everything I want."* With that last truthful admission, Tallon seemed rather shocked.

Sloan stroked his neck. The blood had dried where her nails had dragged over the length of his throat. Unfortunately, it had been the only successful strike she'd made before he'd bound her arms and thrown her into the vehicle.

"Fine." Sloan shifted the pistol in Tallon's direction and moved out from behind the protective barrier of the table. "You can soften the bitch up for me. I'll take my turn after you. I'd enjoy that." He smiled obscenely, revealing his perverse obsession with Tallon.

Tallon hurled himself across the room, driving Sloan into the wall. Loosened plaster fell to the floor. With one big hand tightening around Sloan's throat, he slammed Sloan's wrist against the wall. Using the heel of his free hand, Sloan bashed Tallon's temple. Tallon reeled, his grip loosening on Sloan's throat. Sloan managed to scrape his bloodied hand up the wall and take aim at Tess again.

The liquor had made the gun seem a vague irritation, but the murderous look on Sloan's face made it suddenly all too real. Tess's pulse pounded thickly in her ears.

Immediately, Tallon released his hold on Sloan, and, with hands held up in a placating gesture, he backed away.

Sloan used the gun as a prod in Tallon's chest and forced him across the room. Tess rose noiselessly from her chair, stretched over the table and snatched up a dagger. She cupped it carefully between her hands and settled back on her seat.

Tallon's calves collided with the settee and he fell back onto the cushions.

Without turning his back on Tallon, Sloan returned to his seat at the table. "Seduce the bastard," he ordered Tess. Sloan's eyes had an unnatural gleam. His anticipation was palpable.

Tess wanted Tallon so desperately, she was willing to do Sloan's bidding. It did not matter that Sloan watched, it only mattered that Tallon was there. The short walk to the settee made her head spin, and without her hands to steady her, she felt as if she were tipped at an angle. Still cradling the small dagger in her hands, she awkwardly straddled her husband's leg, her skirts falling on either side of his thigh. As she toppled forward, he wrapped his hands around her arms and propped her up.

Tess did what her body demanded. With her knees braced on the couch, she rubbed along the hard muscles of his thigh. His leather riding breeches felt exhilarating against the soft folds of her sex.

Discreetly, she shifted her eyes in Sloan's direction. "Promise me you will put me out of my misery before he lays a finger on me," she said in a quavering whisper and parted her palms, giving him a peek at what she held.

Tallon's fingers tightened, viselike around her arms, his eyes glossed with what she suspected were tears. "We'll finish this later, love," he said, and plunked her onto the settee beside him. He plucked the dagger from her hands, whipped around and sent the blade whirring through the air. It planted itself in Sloan's shoulder.

Tallon ran at the table and shoved it with bone-crunching power into Sloan's ribs before throwing it off him, overturning the table. The weaponry clattered to the floor, the bottle shattered, spilling its vile green contents. Tallon crashed a fist straight into his face. He landed two more brutal punches in quick succession. Blood poured from Sloan's nose and mouth as Tallon grabbed his shirt, lifted him from the chair and hurled him to the ground.

"I may need this." Tallon bent over Sloan's prone body and wrenched out the dagger.

Sloan screamed out in agony.

Tallon wiped the blade clean on Sloan's shirt before slipping the weapon back into his boot.

Tess's head spun as she stood. Having to look up at her tall husband's face made her dizzier. She swayed, and he grabbed her arm to steady her.

"You realize I want you more than ever now," she said.

"I thought as much," he drawled.

"Shouldn't we be leaving?" Standing on tiptoes, she looped her tied hands around his neck and pressed her breasts against his hard chest. A dimple creased his cheek.

His big hand squeezed her bottom. "Patience, rabbit. I need to drag this worthless devil to the constable's."

"But you never found the counterfeit money."

"It hardly matters, considering the man just kidnapped my wife. It's about time he learns what the inside of a prison is like."

He untied the bonds around her wrists and used the ropes to secure Sloan's hands.

Tallon straightened and turned back to Tess. In an instant, she was clinging to him again. "You've buttoned your waistcoat wrong," she said with a laugh.

"I left in a bit of a hurry."

She could not seem to focus. Her attention strayed to the strong line of his jaw and she reached up to trace it with her fingertips.

"I've only my horse, so you must stay here."

Fascinated, she watched as his Adam's apple bobbed as he spoke. "Tess, sweeting, promise you will not step one foot out that door." He grabbed her arms and gave her a gentle shake.

"I promise." Tess wanted him with such intensity that she nearly cried.

Tallon turned around and hauled Sloan to his feet.

Sloan tried unsuccessfully to twist free. "Hell-born bastard."

Tallon propelled Sloan forward with a shove. "Move."

Left alone, Tess did not know what to do with herself. Hoping to find relief from the heat building inside her, she moved to the window. She pressed her cheek against the cool glass. From this angle she could see the tall mast of what she surmised was Sloan's ship. Tallon had saved her from a horrific fate. Yet she felt an overwhelming sense of sadness. How she wished he had married her under different circumstances. Not to keep her from Sloan's clutches, not just to have her in his bed, but because he truly loved her.

Fog was creeping in from the shore. Soon the cottage would be enveloped in mist. She prayed Tallon would make it back safely tonight.

Not wishing to stay alone in a dark cottage, she went in search of candles. In a cabinet that held wine bottles and little else, she found an oil lamp and a tinderbox.

Comforted by the light the lamp provided, she decided to explore the rest of the small dwelling. The walls were painted a cream color and still smelled of fresh paint. She opened the door onto the only other room. A canopied bed with a crimson satin quilt took up nearly the entire space. Squeezed into a corner was a chair upholstered in the same red satin. The only other piece of furniture was a peculiar little marble-topped stand. The cottage would have been their destination after their elopement. Would Sloan have created this brothel-like atmosphere if she had not insulted him in the garden by murmuring Tallon's name? If he had still thought her the chaste daughter of a viscount? Even then, Sloan's façade would not have held for long. The man's true nature would have shown itself eventually.

Tess ran her fingers down one of the smooth wood posts of the bedstead. She kicked off her slippers and curled her toes in the lushly thick rug on the floor. After setting the oil lamp atop the marble stand, she stretched out on the soft mattress. The silken material felt utterly sensual against her skin. She hoped rest would weaken the desire that raged through her.

Tess started at the sound of a door slamming. Tallon shouted her name. He sounded panicked. She meant to respond, but her thoughts wouldn't translate into words. Her head was still clouded with dreams of him, her limbs felt luxuriously heavy. Turning her face, she watched the door, waiting for him to find her. She heard him stumble his way through the dark. There would only be the thin light coming from beneath the bedroom door to guide him.

He made another crashing entrance. As he approached, she noticed the hitch in his step. Obviously, today's adventure had aggravated his war wound.

"Why the devil didn't you answer me?"

She slid off the bed, planting herself right in front of him. To balance herself, she clutched his lapels for support. "I'm sorry. I cannot seem to do exactly what my mind wishes me to do."

"Forgive me. Your vanishing this morning has unsettled me."

The man had absolutely no idea how much she loved him.

She traced from the white scar that bisected his eyebrow to his strong jaw. Her fingers enjoyed the feel of the blue-black stubble that shadowed his face. "You didn't shave."

"As I said, I was a tad rushed this morning." He scrutinized her. "Cyrus is bringing the carriage, but he's probably still hours away. We'll be staying here tonight."

That's a good thing, she thought. She'd make a bloody fool of herself crawling all over him within the confines of the carriage. She moved her fingers to his lips so she could feel him speak. The warmth of his breath sent a tingle snaking down her back. Her craving for him was spiraling out of her control. She needed to put some distance between them. The impulses became stronger with each passing minute. If he didn't leave soon she would be pleading with him and the thought embarrassed her.

"Perhaps you'd like some wine? Sloan won't have any use for it in Newgate. He has a stash of bottles in the cabinet out there." She held the lamp out to him and gently nudged him toward the door.

"Are you trying to get rid of me?"

"Yes, actually."

He looked completely confused and quite hurt. Could she blame him? Here she was stroking him at the same time she was coaxing him to leave.

After shutting the door on him, she worked the latch into a locked position. Tess felt her way through the dark and with some effort turned the chair to face the wall. Fearing that these sexual cravings would shock even a man as worldly as her husband, she settled onto the satin cushion determined to please herself. With her feet placed on the chair's edge, she shoved her skirts above her hips and spread her knees wide. Closing her eyes, she slid her hand down to her quim.

She registered the sound of cracking wood, the flickering of the lamplight on the ceiling, but she continued to slide her fingers over her exposed wet quim, desperate to assuage the hunger.

"Starting without me, I see." Feeling his heated gaze boring into her, she tilted her head back to find him towering over her. She lifted her bottom to give him a better view and slipped a second finger into herself. With muscles bulging, he lifted the chair off the ground and turned it to face forward. She could not miss his massive erection. With a moan, she stuck another finger deep inside herself. He wrapped his hands around her ankles and dropped them one at a time over the arms of the chair, spreading her so far apart that her muscles hummed in her thighs.

"My turn."

She removed her fingers only to have them replaced by his. First two then three of his big, callused fingers plunged inside her. Mesmerized by his fingers thrusting in and out of her, she obeyed readily when he told her to remove her dress. She slipped it off her shoulders and began working loose the ties of her stays. Every time she would shift to get a better reach behind her, it would cause his fingers to delve deeper. Finally, she yanked off her stays, and her breasts popped free. Her nipples stood hard, eager to be touched. She cupped her hands under her breasts and lifted them for his delectation.

He reached out and rubbed a nipple between his fingers. She moaned in delight. With fingers still thrusting hard into her, he leaned over her and sucked her nipple between his teeth. He lavished the same attention on her other breast. When he lifted his head, her nipples, glossed with his kisses, puckered in the cool air.

He took her hand and tugged her out of the chair. "Get all

your damn clothes off," he demanded and started shedding his own. But she was faster. He had only managed to remove his coat and waistcoat, while she was pushing the last of her petticoats from her hips. He stopped with his hands on his buttons, his lids heavy with desire as he watched her climb naked atop the bed.

The bedstead was fashioned from beautiful blonde wood. The wood was as smooth as glass and carved into a very suggestive shape. At least suggestive to her aphrodisiac-soaked brain. On impulse, her hands curled around the bedpost. Watching him all the while, she suggestively slid her hands up and down the smooth pole. Her actions elicited a groan from deep in his throat. Wishing to provoke him further, she got to her feet and pressed her quim against the cool wood. With a breathy sigh, she shimmied down the length of the post until her bottom rested on her heels.

"Woman, what are you doing to me? You've got that poison Sloan fed you raging through your veins. Yet look at me." He held out his hands. They were trembling. "I've never wanted anything so much in my life."

"Your hands are trembling but my entire being is on fire," she said with a nervous giggle.

She swung off the bed and went to him. Pressing her open mouth to the sleek skin of his muscular chest, she unfastened his trousers. She slid down the length of him, trailing kisses over his stomach as she smoothed his trousers down his legs. When his cock sprang free, her mouth was instantly on it. Her tongue licked the length of the ridge then swirled around the fleshy head, her hands gently squeezing the velvety sacs. His fingers dug into her curls, and he pulled her upward. His chest heaved as he scooped her into his arms and set her hard atop the small stand, which was braced against the wall.

"Ingenious bastard. Sloan had this piece of furniture built for this very thing."

Why hadn't she noticed that before? The marble top had been carved to cradle a woman's buttocks perfectly. And when Tess parted her thighs, she noticed that the front of the stand had been cut away to allow deeper penetration by the male.

His thumb rubbed along her slit. "Had this cottage filled with everything he'd need to give his wife, *my wife*, a thorough fucking." His midnight blue eyes flashed fiercely.

"Mm. A thorough fucking. I want that." She leaned back against the wall.

With utter fascination, she watched him plunge into her. She gripped the edges of the stand as her body absorbed stroke after masterful stroke. But it wasn't enough. Her body craved closer contact with him. She wanted to feel more of his skin against hers. As if he'd read her mind, he lifted her from the table and tossed her on the mattress. He flung the two pillows that were blocking his path to her. One struck the bedpost and the contents spewed out. Counterfeit banknotes littered the bed and floor like confetti.

"Sloan's money." She moved to retrieve the notes, but he snatched her back.

"We've got more important things to take care of." He bent her down over the bed and placed a constraining hand at the nape of her neck. Delirious with need, she twitched her bottom at him and listened with satisfaction to his groan. He thrust into her hard, bringing her to her toes. She pushed her face into the bedclothes to muffle a cry. His hand rubbed roughly over the length of her back. With both hands, he took hold of her bottom, lifting it so he could bury himself deeper still. And she found herself responding, opening herself to him, rocking against him. He repeated her name over and over, his voice heavy with need as he filled her with his seed.

She felt fidgety, as if all her nerves were tingling. All she could think was—*I want more, more, more.* She squirmed from his grasp. His hand shot out to grab her back, but she took a seat on the edge of the bed and wrapped herself in the quilt.

There was tension in the set of his broad shoulders as he left the room. He returned with a bottle of wine dangling from his fingers. He threw aside the cork and took a drink straight from the bottle. A red drop glistened on his bottom lip, which he wiped away with the back of his hand.

The intensity of his scrutiny unsettled her. "I haven't satisfied you yet."

"I don't think it's possible."

He continued to take swigs of wine. For a long while they regarded each other in uneasy silence. When he finally set the bottle down, only half the contents remained. "Then you won't mind if I satisfy myself. Again."

"Are you trying to be amusing, Tallon?" She laughed. "You know I would not deny you anything you wished tonight."

"We'll see," he said, his words a dare. "I want you on your hands and knees there." He pointed to a spot on the floor.

There was no question who was in control of the situation now. Was he taking the fact that she hadn't found release as a challenge? She quickly rejected that notion. There was a predatory, possessive hunger in the way he was regarding her. He was doing this for himself. The want in his eyes was startling. She hesitated a moment, and he tore the quilt from her hands. Her body trembled in anticipation as she got into the vulnerable position on the rug at his feet. Would he take her from behind again?

He dropped to his knees between her spread legs and stroked her moist, heated cleft with the full length of his cock. A shock ran through her when he pressed the tip tentatively to her anus. Yes. She wanted that. Something deeper, more extreme, more intimate. She rested her face against the soft rug and placed her hands on her buttock cheeks and parted them in invitation. He drew his thumb over her tight, puckered opening. And then he tested her, inserting a finger he'd moistened with her own cream. She jolted a bit at the pressure of his finger inside her.

Tess felt him shift position, push himself away a bit. She worried that because of her startled reaction he would find some gentlemanly reason why he couldn't possibly continue— but instead he placed his hands over hers and spread her cheeks farther apart. She shivered with delight as he leaned over and roughly traced the rim with his tongue. He was getting her wet and ready for him. Then he settled himself between her spread legs again and took hold of her hips, tilting them upward for a better angle. Tess removed her hands from her bottom and used them as a cushion for her face. She held her breath as he pressed the fleshy head against her tight opening. Involuntarily, her body clenched against the coming intrusion. Her legs were shaking.

"Relax, love." His deep voice seemed to resonate through her.

Tess shut her eyes and told herself to calm down. But her pulse continued to hammer in her ears. She could sense the restraint in his movements as he entered her slowly. His cock felt amazingly hard and impossibly big. An unfamiliar cry escaped her lips as she responded to the pain and pleasure of what he was doing to her. His hands tightened on her hips as he controlled his movements. He was being *too* careful.

"Please. I want more," she begged. Pressing herself against the floor to give herself some leverage, she pushed back onto his hardness until she could feel his balls against her wet quim.

"Fuck me," she said bucking against him, letting him know that she was relishing the experience. He soon set up a breath-stealing rhythm. The pain never completely faded, but it was overwhelmed by the wickedly delectable sensation of each thick, invasive stroke. He moved his hand from her hip and slipped it down to her nether lips. Finding her nub, he teased it between his finger and his thumb. His skillful manipulation of her quim and his deep thrusts from behind soon brought her to the brink. She was joined to the man she loved in a wildly intimate way. The feeling was incredible. Her quim clenched tight and green sparks the color of the bizarre liquor burst behind her eyelids.

She clutched at the rug as she came to an indescribably sweet climax. He collapsed heavily atop her, his warm breath against the nape of her neck as he shuddered inside of her.

"Tess, my love, you've done me in." He reached up and yanked the quilt from the bed to cover them.

She shifted out from beneath his solid body. He flopped onto his back, scooped her up and settled her atop him. Tess nestled her face in the hollow of his chest. The glints of green were just beginning to fade when she drifted off to sleep.

∞

Unable to open her eyes fully, Tess raised herself on her forearms and squinted down at her husband. His hands were stacked behind his head and he was staring up at her. Uneasy, she climbed off him and stood with care. Feeling fragile, Tess moved cautiously around the room and retrieved her discarded clothing from the floor. She dragged the chemise over her head. Even the soft fabric of the shift felt rough against her sensitive skin.

"I'm off to find where John parked the carriage overnight," Tallon said.

Tess turned and found that he was completely clad and already shrugging into his coat, while she was still attempting to fasten her stays.

He watched her struggle with the laces. "Could you use some help?"

She refused his offer with a shy shake of her head.

Soon after he'd left, Tess heard the creaking of harness and the wheels of the carriage on the unpaved road outside the cottage. After combing her fingers through her tangled hair, she wrapped herself in his greatcoat and stepped outside to face the day. The thin, gray light seemed to pierce her head. She narrowed her eyes at the assault and pressed her fingers to her temples. Her hands were shaking from the effects of the drugs wearing off.

Her bed partner, on the other hand, looked quite well-rested despite spending such an active night. He smoothed back an errant lock of black hair from his brow. For an unobstructed view of her, she surmised. His intense gaze was trained on her again just as it had been earlier when she'd awoken atop him.

Tess greeted Cyrus who sat beside John the driver atop the box of the sleek coach. A large gray horse was tethered to the back of the coach.

"Where's your stallion?" she asked.

"Dante abhors London. I would have lost time fetching him from the country."

"Lord Marcliffe rode like a madman," the driver said with a chuckle as he opened the coach door for her. "I hadn't a chance of keeping up with him."

Once inside, she slid across the bench, retreating from her husband, tucking into a shaded corner of the carriage. There was something disconcerting in the way he stared.

The coach seemed to find every rut in the road. Her brain felt as though it were rattling around in her skull.

"Now that Sloan is finally where he belongs there is no longer any reason—" She jolted upright as his fist slammed into the side of the carriage.

"Do not dare utter a word about leaving me. Will you still see me suffer for tricking you into marriage? Have you not had enough of revenge? Do you wish to destroy me as well?"

"If you'd only let me finish."

"You are bound to me for life," he interjected forcefully. "You are my wife. My only love."

A sudden sob escaped her lips. She tried unsuccessfully to muffle it in the sleeve of the greatcoat. Joy and relief surged through her.

"Bloody wonderful. The thought of staying married to me brings you to tears."

"I was about to say that there is no longer any reason to remain in London. I am anxious to see your manor in—where is it? Essex or Sussex?"

"Actually, I have one in both," he answered dryly.

"Oh," she said with a tiny squeak of delight. "Both."

Tallon unclenched his fists, and his shoulders relaxed. But he rubbed his hands on his trousers as though his palms were sweating. Clearly, something still troubled him.

Tess idly twirled a coil of her hair around her finger and studied him. "In the end, the scheme paid off quite handsomely."

"Really?"

"Well, there's one bad man in prison and one *very bad* man in my bed."

"Must I remind you that you were nearly killed?"

"I will admit there were a few snags."

"Last night was curious," he said abruptly.

A blush crept up her cheeks. Curious, indeed, to have your new bride slide down a bedpost to stimulate her cunt, to use his term, or get down on all fours and beg to be fucked. "How do you mean?" she dared to ask, hoping he wouldn't embarrass her by bringing up something outrageous she'd said or done.

"Never once did you utter a romantic sentiment. No whispered words of love. The alcohol and herbs had stripped you of inhibitions, yet you hadn't anything heartfelt to say to me."

"My mouth was rather occupied."

"It isn't now," he said dryly.

"Oh, but it could be."

He shifted uncomfortably, tugging at his trousers. Her words were making him hard. "I would have thought those substances would have worn off by now."

"They have."

He regarded her suspiciously from beneath his lowered lids. "Your lips are still swollen from last night, yet you would kneel for me? Why?"

"Purely out of desire for the man I love."

"No doubt you are taking pity on me. Hell, I practically begged you to say that." He plucked her off the seat and placed her on his lap. She rubbed her cheek against his unshaven face. She could feel the muscle in his jaw working.

He slipped his hand beneath her neckline and pulled the necklace from her cleavage. He slid the ring onto his finger.

"You have been so blinded by your thoughts of revenge you have barely noticed me. Perhaps, now that this is behind us, you could try to devote a bit of thought to your husband."

Incredulous, she set her hands on his shoulders and held herself away so she could look directly into his eyes. "Now that may be a little difficult to manage. Sparing a bit of time for you, I mean. Considering that I bloody well think of you all day long as it is."

"Is that true?" His captivating dimple made an appearance.

She smiled. "Too true. I love you, Tallon."

"By God, I have missed that dazzling smile." He pressed her hand to his heart. She could feel it pounding against her palm.

Nestling snug against his chest, she tucked her head beneath his chin. "This is what happiness feels like. It's been so long, I'd almost forgotten."

About the Author

To learn more about Scottie Barrett, please visit www.scottiebarrett.com. Send an email to Scottie at scottie@scottiebarrett.com.

What is a lady to do when her chosen rake changes her lessons in seduction to lessons of love?

Lessons in Seduction
© 2007 Melissa Schroeder

Cicely Ware understands how society works. At the age of twenty-six, she has been around long enough to know that she is doomed to spinsterhood. But she refuses to go without ever knowing what it is like to be with a man. So she comes up with a wonderful plan to find a rake to teach her, complete with a list of possibilities. At the top of that list sits Douglas the Duke of Ethingham.

When he asks Lady Cicely to waltz, Douglas never expected her to request seduction, or that it would intrigue him quite as much. With each glance, each smile, each touch, he finds himself falling under her spell, unable to resist her lure. In her he finds a soul mate, someone as lonely as he is, who understands his pain, and will give herself to him without demands or expectations.

But as he finds himself falling in love, he also discovers a wicked plot to kill Lady Cicely. As they race to discover who wants her dead, they fall deeper in love, leaving them to decide if the lessons in seduction could lead to a lifetime of happiness.

Available now in ebook and print from Samhain Publishing.

Enjoy the following excerpt from Lessons in Seduction...

The room that Douglas had in mind was indeed perfect for seduction, thought Cicely. A branch of candles cast dancing shadows along the walls, and a fire had been lit. The coziness of the room made her think that their hosts had left it to welcome liaisons.

The click of the door lock caused Cicely's heart to jump a bit. She was not sure what Douglas had in mind for tonight, but a strange mixture of apprehension and anticipation wound through her.

She did not turn around as Douglas moved toward her. He stepped up behind her, sliding his arms around her waist and drawing her against him. His body heat warmed her but she shivered. Not because she was cold but because he was doing absolutely delicious things with his lips to her neck.

He chuckled, his breath feathering over her skin. "Like that?"

She nodded, then bent her head to the side to allow him more access. His lips moved over her, nipping and licking. His teeth grazed the sensitive flesh just behind her earlobe.

"What did you have in mind tonight, Douglas?"

He paused and slowly turned her around. "I think it is better if I surprise you."

Pulling her close, he took her mouth in a kiss that spoke of not only passion, but possession. She twined her arms behind his head as his hands slipped around her waist and pressed her against his aroused body. When she felt his hands on her bottom, she gasped, and he used the opportunity to invade and conquer. His tongue tangled with hers, a dance of seduction on another level.

Just as the night at the theater, her body reacted on some primitive level she did not fully comprehend. Her flesh grew damp and her nipples hardened—begging to be caressed. As if he heard her thoughts, he moved from her mouth to her throat, nipping and kissing until he reached her neckline. Baring her breasts, he skimmed his mouth over them, arousing one, then the other. With each touch of his tongue to her flesh she lost another bit of her grip on reality.

In the next moment, her world turned on its axis as Douglas lifted her and placed her on the desk. Before she could understand what was happening, he was pulling away from her, getting down onto his knees in front of her.

"Douglas?"

He smiled. "Trust me, love."

She pulled her lower lip between her teeth and nodded. Without taking his gaze from hers, he grabbed hold of the skirt and slowly eased it up her legs. His palms followed the silk, skimming along her thighs. Her heart was now beating out of control, her face burning with embarrassment. But she refused to look away. Instead, she held his gaze boldly. At that, his smile widened, warmed. Mesmerized by it, and the corresponding heat in his eyes, she did not realize at first he was sliding her legs apart and slipping in between them. Before she could react, he bent his head and pressed a kiss on her inner thigh.

Heat shot to molten lava within her veins. She opened her mouth to reject this action, to tell him it was not right. What she had wanted to say dissolved the moment his tongue skimmed the skin just above her stocking. Her senses thrilled, her nerve endings danced. The scrape of teeth, the swipe of his tongue, he continued his actions as he moved up her leg.

Closing her eyes, she ignored the rising physical discomfort that had her wanting to stop this insanity. But somewhere, somehow, she knew it would cause more pain to stop.

He carried on with his assault until he reached the apex of her thighs. Alarm shot through her as she felt his breath on the most private part of her body. Her eyes flew open, her mouth followed to reprimand him. She was wet there, her body melting under his masterful assault, but when she gathered her wits and tried to close her legs, he ignored her. She expected him to comfort her, tell her not to worry, but he seemed transfixed. Without a word, he pressed his mouth against her.

"Douglas!"

He did not even flinch at her shout. Instead, he applied himself to licking, touching and kissing her intimately. Her breasts ached, her body throbbed. Cicely knew she should stop him. What he was doing was not right, could not be right. But the warmth of his mouth had her softening to his demands. He positioned his hands beneath her bottom and pulled her closer, feasting on her as if she were his last meal.

Not able to speak, not willing to ruin the delicious decadence he worked on her, she closed her eyes again. His fingers dug into her rear end as he persisted. His siege against her senses toppled every defense she had against him. Her body tightened, wet heat surged. Fire blazed a path along her flesh.

The muscles that had tensed now grew almost unbearably tighter. She shook her head, trying to grab control of her sanity, but he continued. His mouth grew more insistent as he worked, and her body responded. Nerves grew taut and she felt like she was racing toward a goal she did not know or understand. And still, he continued. His hands were moving over the globes of her rear end, her skin putty beneath his palms. Smoothly, easily, he pushed her, prodded her to the finish. Understanding that he would catch her, that he knew just what she needed, she surrendered—her body, her soul—to the pleasure that called to her.

GREAT
CHEAP
FUN

Discover eBooks!

THE FASTEST WAY TO GET THE HOTTEST NAMES

Get your favorite authors on your favorite reader, long before they're
out in print! Ebooks from Samhain go wherever you go, and work with
whatever you carry—Palm, PDF, Mobi, and more.

SAMHAIN
PUBLISHING LTD

WWW.SAMHAINPUBLISHING.COM

CPSIA information can be obtained at www.ICGtesting.com
Printed in the USA
LVOW040836140412

277620LV00001B/64/P